To Jace,

ONE DAY AT CHRISTMAS

Keep Christmas in your heart!

Virginia

Virginia Nolan
and
Michael Fedele

ISBN: 1539381013
ISBN 13: 9781539381013
Library of Congress Control Number: 2016916904
Createspace Independent Publishing Platform
North Charleston, South Carolina

CHAPTER ONE

W hile sitting on the edge of his bed, Jack leaned forward. His huge, calloused hands reached out as if drawn to a magnet. On the top right-hand corner of his desk sat the snow globe that he had treasured for years. Jack cupped his palms around the coolness of the glass and once again felt comforted.

Yes, there had to be a way, he thought. As he tipped the snow globe to its side, the flakes began to swirl. Jack sat motionless, waiting for the energy to transmit into his veins. A new day was unfolding whether he liked it or not.

Jack returned the snow globe to its designated spot. Patiently, he watched as the flakes began to settle. It had become a daily routine. Today, he was betting that most of the snow would settle on the toy-filled sack. The second runner-up would be the black boots, and in third place, the shoulders of the red suit. It was always a gamble; life was a gamble.

Wouldn't it be great if I could just shake off the worries like the flakes within the globe?

The problems of others entered without permission and constantly swirled in his head.

Once again, Jack had beaten the piercing buzz of his radio alarm clock, set for the usual 5:30 a.m. Automatically, he switched on his preset news station. "Only twenty-three more days till Christmas."

While listening, Jack gave the globe another shake. He continued to be mesmerized by the flakes as they found their respective niches. *Only twenty-three days...*

Jack's broad brow furrowed as his dark brown eyes traveled from the globe to the calendar that hung above his desk. Each day of the week had penciled reminders waiting to be checked off. Today, the recyclables had to be brought to the curb for early morning pickup.

Only twenty-three more days...

Anxiously, he reached for the snow globe again, turned it over, and wound it. Thoughts tumbled in his head to the tune of "Jingle Bells." Flashing scenes of children tearing opening presents ran rampant in his brain; as the music waned, his heart rate struggled to reset to its normal pace.

"Hey, Mr. L., you in there?"

"Yeah, I'll be right there," Jack bellowed back. He sensed the loud, desperate tone of the voice that had accompanied the frantic knock. Quickly, Jack returned the globe to its resting spot as it finished the last few dying notes and rushed to open the outside door.

"What's the matter, Joe?"

"We have no heat again in apartment 3C."

"Sorry about that. I'll get right on it."

"Thanks, Mr. L. The baby's got a cold, and the weather is lousy. Supposed to get some freezing rain and snow. My wife will be home if you need to get into the apartment. I've got to get into work early today. A little extra cash always helps at this time of year."

"I know what you mean. I'll take a look at the old boiler and hopefully will be able to get it crankin' again. Maybe the radiators need to be bled. I'll check it out. Don't you worry about it, Joe. I'll take care of it. Have a good day."

Knowing that Jack would take care of it was one of the good things that came with living in that apartment house. Jack was a good super, and the tenants of 649 Longwood knew they could count on him.

As Jack shook his hand, the stress lines on Joe's brow softened. Relieved, Joe quickly turned and hastened to catch the Lexington Avenue 6 train. His job at the Cooperative Market in the South Bronx was hard work, but it put food on their table and paid the rent.

Have a good day... Yeah, that's what everyone says, thought Joe, as he headed for the subway to get to work. An extra few hours added to his time sheet would boost his weekly paycheck. Maybe he could slowly dig himself out of the ditch that he was in.

Joe had lived at 649 Longwood for eleven years. He had moved in with his new bride, Anita, right after Jack La Falla had taken over the job as building superintendent. Joey came along soon after, and Jasmine arrived when Joey was only two. Now with the new, unexpected baby, things were really tight in their four-room apartment—not only in square footage but financially as well.

Anita suffered from migraines and hadn't worked since Miguel had arrived. In apartment 3C, stress hovered like a low-flying kite, taking a nose dive at times while still allowing miniscule bits of hope to spike the atmosphere. But maybe that wasn't the only place tension prevailed in the building. The general hallway traffic that offered the "Hi, have a good day, hope it doesn't rain/ snow" kind of daily greeting, contrasted with the slammed doors, yells, screams, and stomping of everyday frustrations. Jack had a keen sense of what caused the dynamics of the building. He was a good listener and observer. Because the tenants trusted Jack, they often shared their thoughts.

With the second job, Joe's secret plan was to buy a small house in the Pelham Bay section of the Bronx. He wanted a better neighborhood and school district for his kids. He silently hummed the tune "To dream the impossible dream" from *Man of La Mancha* as he headed to the subway.

Jack didn't skip a beat. He was on a mission. So he dressed quickly and snatched the warm, quilted, dark gray work jacket that hung on the hook next to the door to the outside. He headed immediately to the boiler room at the rear of the red brick building.

Even though the boiler had been serviced at the beginning of November, it sometimes needed a little friendly persuasion. Jack knew its hum, its cough, and its kick. It was like his baby that always demanded his attention.

Yes, that was only one of many things that demanded his attention. Lately, his brain seemed to be on constant overload. The tenants of these fifteen apartments in this low-income building were like family to him, and he aimed to please.

CHAPTER TWO

Shortly after Thanksgiving, the countdown to Christmas began. For Jack, this was the season when memories flickered like candles on a cold, windy night. At the young age of fifteen, being able to join Dad after school at a neighborhood job had always been a thrill for Jack.

"See, the consistency of the mortar has to be just right, so the bricks will adhere properly." Jack listened and watched in awe as his dad flicked the trowel. "Here, Jack, you try." Watching and doing were two different things. "You'll get it. Practice makes perfect."

They started to reminisce about Jack's early years, as they continued to lay the top layer of bricks on the outer wall of the rooftop. "Remember when you hit that home run in Little League, son? Everyone cheered, and you won the game for the team. I always told you to give it your personal best, and you did." Jack loved the time alone with his dad and treasured his words of wisdom.

"Well, it's getting late." Neither of them wore a wristwatch for fear of ruining it. The street lights just came on. That was always the signal to head home.

"I can help you finish up, Dad."

"No, get going and tell Mom I'll be home in about fifteen minutes."

"OK."

Aiming to please, Jack put down the trowel, descended the five flights of stairs to the street, and jogged home. He anticipated the wonderful aroma of Mom's home cooking.

He burst in the door, announcing, "Dad says he'll be home in about fifteen minutes, Mom."

"Good. Now go set the table so we can eat as soon as your father arrives."

Jack was the oldest and always tried to be obedient. Now, at a different stage of life, responsibilities seemed to weigh Jack down like leaded shoulder pads. They stretched far beyond the maintenance of the building.

Little League was no longer his game. Jack could still picture his dad standing on the sidelines, cheering him on. After a loss, his dad would put a hand on his shoulder and try to cheer him up. "Listen, son, it doesn't matter if you win or lose; it's how you play the game."

CHAPTER THREE

*P*lay the game... Yeah, thought Jack. *This Christmas, I'm gonna use a different strategy, and hopefully it'll work.* Thoughts continued to tumble. *Careful planning, yeah, that's it. I'll give it my personal best. I've got lots of people here who need some cheering up.*

Tillie Bauer was at her kitchen window, checking out the usual Monday morning activities. After fixing the boiler, Jack gave an upward glance as he began to take the cans from the side yard to the front curb for the NYC sanitation curbside pickup. *Yep, she's up bright and early. Good sign.*

This had been Jack's way of silently keeping tabs on her ever since her husband Karl passed away two years ago. She was thought to be somewhere in her eighties now. The exact age had never been revealed in the twelve years that Jack had been there. Tillie's husband always used to say, "Age is only a number, and mine is unlisted." She continued to think in the same way. Karl's tombstone read BELOVED HUSBAND, September 12, 1998. His year of birth was never revealed.

Since the Bauers had no children of their own, Joey and Jasmine had become their adopted grandchildren. Now that Karl was gone, Tillie would anxiously await their return from school each day at 3:10 and would leave the door to her apartment, 2A, open a crack.

"*Yoo-hoo*," she'd call in her sweet, Alpine yodel of a voice. When they heard that call, Joey and Jasmine always knew there'd be a treat waiting for them and would rush up the stairs and peek in to say hello. It often turned out to be a tea party. If Tillie wasn't up to baking, the children knew where she kept the secret stash of candy kisses.

Mrs. Bauer came from the old school. She never believed in the store-bought variety of cake and cookies. At least twice a week, the aroma of something baking wafted throughout the building. Jack usually did his sweep of the stairs and hallways in the afternoon. He started at the top and somehow managed to wind up on the second floor about the same time the kids arrived.

"Bring your school bags home, and ask Mom if she'd like to come for tea," Tillie would say. Anita, who was now usually busy with the baby, would seldom come back with them. It was comforting to her to know that her children were in a safe place.

"Jack, why don't you join us?"

The world of fantasy had been sliced out of Jack's life at an early age. The dreary tended to outweigh the happy. When special moments popped up, he lunged for the upward swing.

CHAPTER FOUR

Even though twenty-six years had passed, Jack never forgot that night, that endless wait for Dad to come home. "Wonder where that man is. I hope one of his buddies isn't chewing his ear off or luring him to the pub again," Mom muttered, becoming angrier as the minutes on the clock ticked away.

With the table set, Jack's younger brother and sister sat in front of the TV as the five o'clock evening news began. There were the traditional bell ringers reminding them that there were only ten more days till Christmas. Peggy and Jim watched intently. With Christmas lists in hand, they were sprawled out on the living room floor, adding to their lists for Santa. Hope hovered in the air this time of year, especially in the families who had so little.

"Where is that father of yours?" The frustration emerged in an elevated tone of voice, as their mother ordered them to shut off the TV, sit down, and eat. That night, dinner was quick and silent. There were none of the usual exchanges of everyone's daily events that day.

Everyone in the La Falla household, no matter whether they were six, eight, or fifteen years old, had their jobs. Just as the table was being cleared and the dishes were placed in the sink to be washed, the doorbell rang. "Guess he forgot his key again," Mom exclaimed, as she quickly dried her hands and stomped toward the door.

"I'll get it, Mom," Jack interjected and scurried past her, hoping to ease the anticipated explosion of tension.

Quickly, he unlatched the door. Facing him were two grim-faced policemen. *Oh no, trouble.*

Pushing Jack aside, Mom stepped up to the plate. "Yes, officer?"

"Mrs. La Falla?"

"Yes," she answered hesitantly. The angry tone of voice had vanished.

"May we come in?"

"What's the matter, officer?"

"Can we come in for a moment?"

"Yes, come in. I'm expecting my husband any moment."

She gestured toward the living room. "Please sit."

"I think you'd better sit down, Mrs. La Falla..."

"What's this about?" she demanded, standing her ground.

"I'm sorry to tell you that your husband is not coming home. There's been a terrible accident."

Trouble would have been easier to digest. I froze. I could hear the words but refused to comprehend.

Jack looked at Mom for help. "What?" she asked.

Her frail body began to tremble as the policemen caught her and led her to the nearby armchair.

That's where Dad should be sitting. My head was spinning like a surreal scene from a movie, images flashed and wailing sounds ensued.

"We'll need you to identify the body," they continued, after explaining his tragic fall from the rooftop staircase of the building where he was working. "It appears that he was carrying down his bundle of tools, slipped, and tumbled down the entire flight of stairs. He must have died instantly, because by the time the medics arrived, there was no heartbeat."

The body…my dad…the body…no! This couldn't be real. They must have the wrong person.

Jack bolted out the door and ran. He needed to escape. Tears streamed down his face as he ran the four blocks to the job site. Everything was roped off. Policemen were surrounding the area. People were out on the street. "Unbelievable"…"How could this have happened?"…."He was such a nice man."

Nice man, thought Jack. *He was my father; he was the best.*

CHAPTER FIVE

All these years, his dad's last words had echoed in his brain like a broken record. "I'll be home in fifteen minutes," continued to haunted him. *What really happened? Maybe if I had stayed, he'd be alive. Why? Why wouldn't he let me stay to help? Why? Why? I should have stayed. I always tried to obey. This time I shouldn't have. If only, if only...*

Every time Jack picked up that glass snow globe, he felt not only soothed but energized as well. As he cupped it in his hands, he focused on the eyes. He could see his father staring back at him. *Dad, Dad...Why did you have to leave me? Help me. Help me do the right thing.*

Jack had treasured that globe since he was six years old. Santa had brought it at Christmastime. Jack remembered walking into the living room, seeing the beautiful, tinseled tree. Underneath its branches were a few presents. One caught his curiosity immediately. It was wrapped in gold paper. He read the tag.

To Jack,
  May all your dreams come true.

Love,
Santa

His dad queried, "What do you think Santa brought you?"

Jack loved guessing. "Maybe blocks?" He shook it. No noise, so he ruled that out. "Maybe a toy truck or a book?" Anticipation got the best of him. He tore the wrapping and slowly opened the cardboard box.

His dad's eyes were on him. "Be careful as you take it out of the box. It could be breakable."

Once it was open, Jack slowly removed the newspaper that surrounded it. His eyes glistened as he held up the glass globe like a trophy. "Look, Dad, look what Santa brought me."

"Wow, you must have been a very good boy," his dad responded, with a great big smile.

"Yes, yes, I guess so," he stammered. He began to examine it. As he turned it over, he discovered it could be wound. "Listen, listen, it's playing 'Jingle Bells,'" he shouted. Jack was thrilled, and they all began to sing. He set the snow globe on the floor and watched the flakes swirl and slowly settle.

The other gifts in the La Falla household were the usual basics—underwear, pajamas, shirts, socks—but every once in a while, there was something special. This present was unique. All these years Jack treasured it and kept it close. The magic of Christmas was always there for Jack, even though his dad was no longer a part of it. Or was he?

CHAPTER SIX

"You don't have to twist my arm, Tillie. I think can manage to spare a half hour."

Tillie's face lit up like a Christmas tree. It was good to see her happy.

Upon returning to Mrs. Bauer's place, Joey and Jasmine spotted the good china cups being carefully taken out of the corner cabinet and set on the silver tray that was placed on the coffee table; they knew they were in for a treat.

"What's the special occasion, Mrs. Bauer?" Not only had the children learned to be extremely careful when the good china was used, but they also knew that it was a day of some importance, personal or nationwide. Anxious to listen, they pulled out the hassocks under the coffee table in the living room and sat quietly in anticipation.

Tillie often revealed stories of the past. When she first decided to use the good stuff, Tillie had told the story about when they had purchased the good china, and how they had to have it shipped back to the United States from Frankfurt, Germany. They used to go back to visit their brothers and sisters. Now life was changed for Tillie; without Karl, that thrill of going back to their homeland in Germany was nonexistent.

"I thought we'd use these cups today because it would have been my fiftieth wedding anniversary." Milk with a little tea was being carefully poured into the Rosenthal china cups. "One lump of sugar or two?" she'd ask, as she passed the bowl filled with cubes of sugar. Joey and Jasmine loved using the silver tongs to procure one cube at a time, plop it into their cups, and then stir gently. Sometimes they pretended to be royalty, lifting their pinky fingers while sipping their tea.

Suddenly, Jack's beeper vibrated in his shirt pocket. He quickly reached for it, took a look at the display, stood up, and declared, "Oh, well, the tea party is over for me. Duty calls. Thanks for the treats. See you later." He saw no need for them to terminate their tea party.

CHAPTER SEVEN

The silent alarm indicator told him it was the storage room. Sometimes kids stole things or just broke into it to hang out; what will it be this time?

Once Jack gently closed the door, he bolted down to the landing between the first and second floors and glanced out the window. Two hooded sweatshirts darting out the back alley caught his attention. His six-foot frame and muscular build was far from dainty as he pounded the marble stair treads to the lobby. Once out the front door, his eyes canvassed the street. He slowed to an inconspicuous walk and cautiously headed to the back of the building. As he turned the corner into the rear of the building, his nose, a built-in smoke detector, told him it wasn't cigarettes or fire. Jack definitely smelled trouble. There was always the decision to be made, call 911 or deal with it alone. After school let out, mischief-makers often appeared.

The door to the storage room was slightly ajar. The hammer that usually rested in his work belt was now in Jack's right hand. He stopped and listened. Seeing no movement, he gingerly pushed open the door and peered into the dark before venturing inside and reaching for the light switch.

"What the—?" Jack bellowed, as he tripped and crashed into the bikes. "Get up, you punk."

The boy didn't budge. Jack nudged him with his foot. The arm covering his face dropped to his chest and both hands went up in self-defense.

Jack, realizing that he was still holding the hammer, put it away. "What are you doing here?"

No response.

He's wasted. Now what? His mother is working and won't be home till late. There's no dad around.

"Get up and help me straighten up these bikes."

A bit shaky, Casey slowly managed to stand. "I'm sorry Mr. L. Really, I'm sorry."

"You'll be sorry all right when I get through with you. Now, give me a hand."

Like a car that was stuck in mud, Casey began to push forward, grab hold, and slowly move to a standing position. Slowly, they untangled the jumble of tires, handlebars, and pedals and positioned the bikes against their kickstands.

After the bikes were lined up and the baby carriages, shovels, brooms, rakes, and tools were straightened, Jack closed the steel door to the storage room and ushered Casey to his office at the front of his apartment.

"Sit there and don't move. You've got a lot of explaining to do before the cops get here."

"Cops? Oh man."

CHAPTER EIGHT

Casey just held his head in his hands while Jack went into his kitchen. He knew he was in trouble. Mr. L. had always been his friend, but now was different. He could tell by the tone of Mr. L.'s voice.

Jack had to get control of his anger before he could talk to Casey. He headed over to the refrigerator, took out a can of beer, and plopped down in exhaustion on the old, wooden chair from his mom's apartment. There he sat in a slouched position, sipping and thinking. The old, beat-up, two-by-four kitchen table, which was hidden behind the office door, was equipped with pads of yellow paper and pencils. The what-to-do list always began here before working its way to the bulletin board. But this afternoon, Jack couldn't jot down anything. His stream of consciousness was dominated by visions of the past.

He pictured himself at fifteen, no longer having a father figure to guide him through the rest of high school. What was worse—a deceased dad or a deadbeat dad? Casey never even talked about his dad, and in the five years Casey and his mother had lived in the apartment house, Jack had never seen nor heard anything about a man in Casey's young life. Kathleen, Casey's mom, was lovely, but she was quiet, had a troubled look in her eyes, and always seemed to be working. Knowing the hell he had faced after his own dad's death enabled Jack to identify with Casey. *This kid needs help.* Jack knew what Casey had not yet learned.

Casey sat on the chair next to Jack's desk in his tiny office just as he was told. While fidgeting in the chair, he kept glancing at the clock on the wall. It was now 4:30 p.m. He was tempted to bolt out the door, but what good would that do? Jack would be on him in a heartbeat. He didn't need more trouble piling up. Were the cops really going to arrive, and what was Jack going to do? Finally, after sitting there for a half hour, which seemed like an eternity, Casey got up the courage to tap lightly on the door to Jack's inner sanctum and sheepishly peek inside.

Jack, motionless at the kitchen table, appeared to be frozen in time. His right thumb and forefinger held his eyes shut. He was leaning back with legs extended.

Casey had never been inside Jack's tiny apartment. Knowing that trespassing on someone else's private domain could be dangerous, Casey proceeded cautiously. "Mr. L., you OK?"

No response.

In a low, unsteady voice Casey managed to utter, "What's the matter, Mr. L.?"

No response. Casey tried for a third time, with a bit of urgency in his voice. "Hey, Mr. L.?" He was watching closely for any signs of movement. He detected very slow breathing. "I'm really sorry I messed up."

Jack had been immobile, struggling to blink back the memories. The inside torture that he had lived with since his dad's death came crashing in like ocean waves on a stormy day. He pictured himself at Casey's age trying to find a way to go forth but often choosing the wrong path.

"Mr. L., I'm really sorry I messed up."

It took several seconds before Jack removed his hand and opened his eyes as if awakened from a dream. Until today, there had always been a good rapport between the two of them. Jack wasn't going to let Casey mess up like he did.

"I know I messed up royally, Mr. L."

Jack finally let his guard down and sat upright, raising his glance to meet the eyes of the young fifteen-year-old standing before him.

Casey, standing there motionless, was unable to read the welled-up tears in Jack's brown eyes.

"Sit," Jack demanded. "We need to talk."

Without hesitation, Casey pulled out the other kitchen chair and sat opposite Jack. "From now on, after school, you'll report to me. I'll assign you jobs here in the building. Got it?"

"Yes sir."

"And if I ever see you smoking that shit again, I will call the cops. Shake yourself free from those dirtbags, and start to get a life for yourself. I won't even ask where you got the money for that junk." Casey listened intently as Jack rambled on; his head hung like a puppy that's been scolded and nodded appropriately as Jack continued to lecture. "Now get upstairs and do your homework so you'll become something other than a loser. I won't tell your mother this time, but if it happens again, I'll throw you under the bus."

CHAPTER NINE

A dismal and bleak atmosphere constantly permeated the air after the death of Jack's father. The funeral and the following days were a blur. Neighbors stopped by, dropped off food, and left. Once the apartment door was closed, you could barely breathe. The air was stagnant. Mrs. L. locked herself in her room, and Jack could hear her cries. He couldn't console her; he needed to be consoled. Peggy and Jimmy clung to him because Mom was unable to function. When they were hungry, they helped themselves to cereal or whatever was available. Christmas was only days away, but it didn't matter. There was no Christmas spirit this year, at least not in the La Falla household.

During the first week after the funeral, Father Murphy, their parish priest and family friend, stopped by every other day after the children came home from school. Usually, he brought a casserole that the parish cook had prepared. His visits were short. He was checking to see if they needed anything and wanted to make sure that there was some food on the table. He knew that Mr. L. had always been the glue that held them together. Mrs. L. uttered a polite "thank you" to him and headed back to the sofa or her bedroom. She claimed to have an upset stomach or a headache each time he came. Father gave her the phone number of a grief counselor, but she never called. She said she needed to wait until she felt better.

Jack opened the mail that came, since his mom just left it un-opened on the table. There was a meager insurance check of ten thousand dollars and a few back paychecks, but this wouldn't last more than three months. After the funeral expenses were paid, there was little left for the basics, rent, and food. Jack knew that he had to find an after-school job.

On Christmas Eve, at 4:00 p.m., the bell rang. Jack, knowing he wasn't supposed to buzz in a stranger, went down the two flights of stairs to see who it was. "Bike delivery for Jack La Falla."

Jack stood there, dumbfounded. "You sure?"

"Yeah. Are you Jack La Falla in apartment 3A?"

"Yes."

"Well, here's the bike that was ordered. Are you gonna accept delivery or not? I've got more to do than just stand here."

Hesitant, Jack couldn't believe what he was hearing. *Bike for me?* It took him a few seconds to collect his thoughts and manage a response. "OK, if it's paid for."

"It's paid for, all right. Where do you want me to leave it?" *Wow, is this guy is for real? He's leaving a bike for me.* Hurriedly, Jack opened the door to the lobby. The delivery guy held the receipt in his hand and was pointing to the name and address on the top. Jack scanned it carefully. There it was, clear as day. Next to the "paid in full" was his father's signature, along with the delivery date, December 24. *That's today.*

"Sign here."

For a moment, Jack stood there, totally dumbfounded. Then he came to his senses, grabbed the pen, and signed below his father's name. The delivery guy tore off the customer's receipt and handed it to Jack. "Here you go. Bye."

"Thanks."

He took the receipt, folded it twice, stuffed it into his pocket, grabbed hold of the handlebars, and sat on the seat with his left foot on the pedal and his right foot on the floor for balance. Unconsciously, Jack blurted out another, "Wow!" This was the bike he and his dad often talked about. This was the someday gift when his dad could afford it, and now it was here. He wasn't going to leave it behind the first-floor staircase as most did. He lugged it up to their third-floor apartment. He was not letting this baby out of his sight. Yes, there is a Santa, he thought.

His heart was racing. Before he entered the apartment, he took a few deep breaths, pulled out the receipt carefully, and took another look. *Am I in a dream warp? Dad?* At the top right-hand corner was the date of sale, December 1, 1982. A fifty-dollar deposit was indicated in the column to the right of the description of the bike. It was paid in full on December 13, just two days before his father's death. His dad had signed next to the "paid in full" at the bottom of the page with the delivery date clearly indicated. He wasn't hallucinating; this was real.

Jack didn't know if his mother knew about this, nor had he ever really thought about what his parents earned or what they could or couldn't afford. There was always food on the table, and they lived in a four-room apartment in the Bronx. When you're fifteen, you really don't know nor do you care about weekly or monthly household expenses. You just asked for money when you really needed it.

Jack had grown up without lots of treats. The only bike he'd ever had was a beat-up hand-me-down given to him by a family whose son had outgrown it. He had been thrilled. Not being used to having a bike, he had left it in front of the building to run upstairs and get a drink. By the time he returned, it was gone. He hadn't been thinking, and he remembered that down-in-the-dumps feeling at having done such a stupid thing. This time, he would make sure that wouldn't happen again.

Slowly, Jack opened the door to the apartment and entered gingerly, not knowing what the reaction would be. There was his mom, sitting in the sofa, watching Peggy and Jimmy sitting on the floor in the center of the living room, playing checkers. Jack couldn't very well hide this new, shiny bike, nor did he want to do so.

"Look what was delivered." Excitement filled the air. With eyes wide, the little ones ran over to inspect the bike.

"Where'd you get it, Jack?"

"Santa's helper just delivered it. What do you think?"

"It's beautiful. Did he bring anything for us?"

"No, I guess you'll have to wait for Christmas morning. This was too big to fit in his sack, don't you think?"

As the kids were examining the bike inch by inch, Jack surveyed his mother's questioning face and headed over to the sofa. He pulled out the pink receipt and unfolded it stealthily, as if he were opening a classified document. He pointed to the signature. "Look, Mom." She tried to focus. "Mom, see."

"Oh, my God." She took her finger and touched the scripted letters as if she were caressing the crown jewels. "It's him." Tears began to flow like penciled waterfalls. "I didn't even know. We both knew you wanted this for a long time, and since you had been working with him, I guess he had put money aside."

"You know what this means, Mom. Now I can get a job. I'll go see Sonny after Christmas and see if he has work for me doing deliveries." Mom reached for his hand. "We're going to be OK. Somehow, I know Dad's looking over us."

She patted his hand tenderly as they sat there watching the pedals spun, the spokes stroked, and the handlebars rubbed by two excited youngsters wondering what their unforeseen gifts from Santa might be.

CHAPTER TEN

Casey knew that Mr. L. meant business. The very next day, he reported right after school as instructed and executed the tasks Jack gave him without the usual teenage groaning and moaning. Casey swept down the five flights of stairs and mopped up each landing just as Mr. L. showed him. "Make sure you get into the corners. This black and white stone tile can be stubborn sometimes. Here, use this spray if there's a tough mark that doesn't come off easily."

"OK."

After about an hour, Casey made his way down to the lobby. "So how'd ya do? Let's check it out." Jack gave the staircase an upward glance and a nod of approval.

"Tomorrow, I'll need help carrying the boxes of decorations out to the lobby. I'd like to have the place decorated by Thursday. So now, you better get upstairs and get crankin' on your homework before your mom arrives. It's almost six o'clock."

"Will do, Mr. L. I'll be here at 3:30 again tomorrow, just like today."

Casey knew there was no choice; Mr. L. had the noose dangling if he stepped out of line. He carried the pail and mop back to the slop sink, rinsed them clean, and stored them. The broom and dust pan were always kept behind the staircase for quick access when needed.

Jack, pleased with his new helper, fastened the eleven-by-fourteen-inch poster-size invitation to the right of the mailboxes with masking tape. Even though invitations had been given to the tenants a week ago, this was a reminder. Jack had taken great pride in doing this for the past five years, and he loved being able to bring some joy into his tenants' lives. Meanwhile, the wheels continued to turn inside his head like a giant bingo roll inside a cage. With the loss of jobs and the economy in bad shape, how could he make this year better?

To: All the Tenants of 649
From: Jack La Falla

The Annual Christmas Gathering will take place on Saturday, Dec. 12
From 10–11:00 a.m.
in the lobby

MENU
Hot Chocolate, Coffee/Tea
Bagels and donuts
and
Tillie's cookies

Hope to see you there.

Kathleen was pleased to see her son sitting at the kitchen table doing his homework when she arrived at the usual 6:30 p.m. She gave him the standard peck on the cheek and pat on the shoulder before taking off her coat. "How was your day?"

The usual "OK" came back.

And so she continued, "Good to see you doing your homework. I guess you're finally growing up, Casey."

Casey just sat there silently with a hint of a smile. He liked pleasing but most often he showed his stubborn streak.

"I had a really tough day today, so it was nice to come home to you being here." Not hassling with him or wondering where he might be hanging out when she got home was a relief. *Wish it would last.*

"Did you see the invitation Jack posted? Hope you'll be around to go."

"Yeah, I think so." *Mom should only know that I have a secret payback contract with Mr. L. Not only am I cleaning, I'm decorating and doing whatever else pops onto his to-do list.*

The next morning after his usual rounds, Jack walked down the block to the local hardware store. He needed to get some more lights, some extra bulbs, and a new extension cord. Every year, he tried to make the Christmas party better than the last.

Pleased with his purchases, he proceeded to the corner candy store.

"Good morning, Frankie. Think we're going to get snow this Christmas?"

"Well, it does feel like it."

"Ya got any of those good cigars I like?"

"Yeah, we just got some in for the holidays. How many d'you want?"

"One will do me for today."

Jack picked up a copy of the Daily News, pocketed his cigar, and paid.

"Have a good day."

"Yeah, you too."

So far, so good. Maybe it will be a good day.

CHAPTER ELEVEN

J ack walked around the corner, sat down at the bus stop bench, and since he had no pressing tasks until this afternoon, decided to enjoy a few puffs.

Holiday music resonated from the nearby stores on the avenue. He was getting into the spirit. Across the street next to the bank was the usual gathering of the red and white suits. Once again, Volunteers of America's sidewalk Santa campaign was gearing up to take its positions around NYC. Their bell ringing had begun on the day after Thanksgiving and continued right up until Christmas Day, helping those in need, including families with hardships, the homeless as well as the homebound. This tradition had been going on every holiday season for more than one hundred years.

Helping, helping, helping—yes! What if...? They wouldn't even know. Nah, too easy. But maybe...nah. It couldn't be that easy.

"You getting on this bus, mister?"

"No, just resting awhile. Thanks."

Jack stubbed out his cigar to save for later, grabbed his bags, and headed back to 649. *It'll be three o'clock before you know it. Wish I had a bag full of money to give out to these families. Boy, could they use it. Maybe I could do a little more this year.*

There were always maintenance repairs in this old apartment house. Jack had his list, and no matter how he tried to keep up, there always seemed to be more. It kept him mighty busy all year round. Busy was good because it gave him a reason to get up and going every morning.

Every once in a while, he got that down-in-the-dumps feeling like being underwater and not being able to surface. For much of his adult life, Jack had been frustrated at not being able to give more of himself. *Maybe I'd be a little bit smarter if I sat in the front of the class instead of the back.*

There was no time for self-pity. The past could not be changed. Jack was on a mission. Casey would not only be his youthful legs but also his secret human reconstruction project. Plans were accelerating at full speed. He just had to be extra careful to not crash. He had done that once in his life and had paid dearly for it.

CHAPTER TWELVE

C asey was put to work the moment he arrived home from school. Jack was already testing the strands of lights to see what worked. His newly purchased supplies were close at hand. "Go get the boxes from the storage room on the back shelves that are marked with a big red *C*. In the back right corner, you'll find the artificial tree wrapped in black plastic. I left the light on 'cause it's kind of dark in there."

"OK, Mr. L."

"I'll set up this stand here and finish testing the lights, while you get all that other stuff. I want to have all these boxes out of the way before the folks start to come home from work."

Casey hustled and carried the six-foot tree into the lobby. It needed a little bit of adjusting after being tied up all winter. Luckily, the tree limbs were still attached, but they definitely needed to be reshaped.

"Where should we put the tree this year?"

"I think last year you had it closer to the front door. Why not put it to the left of the staircase?"

"Good idea. That way the wind won't blow it over when the front door opens." Jack was hoping the "jolly bug" would bite him as well. *Maybe I can make a difference.*

They were both engaged in anchoring the tree, arranging the lights, and putting on the ornaments. The true test would be plugging in the last extension cord. "Go ahead, Casey. I know this isn't the Rockefeller Center tree, but let's give it a go."

"OK, get ready." Casey crouched down behind the staircase with the three-pronged plug in his hand.

Together they counted down: "Five, four, three, two, one." Peeking out from under the staircase was a blondish mop of hair with a disappointed look on his face. "Let me check the cord that feeds into this one."

Jack followed the trail of the extension cord, found the loose plug, and pushed it in tightly.

"OK, let's try it again."

They did the countdown once again. As Casey's head peeked out this time, he was elated. "Wow, we did it!" He jumped out from behind the staircase with a huge grin across his face, admiring the magic of electricity. The explosion of color was overwhelming. One would have thought that they had just won a championship game.

There they were jumping up and down, just as the front door opened and in walked Kathleen, laden with groceries. "Wow! I think you outdid yourself, Jack." It wasn't until she put down her packages that she realized that the person who was giving Jack high-fives was her son.

"Well, well. This is great."

"Yeah, I asked Casey to give me a hand. I'm not as young as I used to be."

Casey froze. Jack did a good cover-up for his new apprentice.

"Hi, Mom. You need a hand with those groceries?"

Some bug had definitely bitten him, and it was wonderful to see the kind, helpful Casey emerge. The proud look on Kathleen's face was enough to make Jack's insides glow as he watched them head toward the stairs.

"See ya, Mr. L."

"Thanks, Casey."

That night, reflecting back on the day's activities, Jack plopped down on the sofa, put on the TV, and finally began to peruse the newspaper he had purchased that morning. This time of year, there seemed to be more ads than news. The discounted prices and special deals always enticed the reader.

This Saturday at the gathering, Jack would play his usual role of Santa and ask the little ones in the building what they'd like Santa to bring them. He'd always appease them and say that sometimes Santa can't bring exactly what they'd like, but that he'd do what he could. Some would leave notes on the tree for Santa with their names and apartment numbers. The magic of believing filled their world at this time of year.

CHAPTER THIRTEEN

Jack's to-do list for the next day or so was always done in the evening.

Thursday:
AM   check out red suit/black boots
       order bagels/donuts for Sat.
       buy hot chocolate packets
            tea bags/coffee
            cream cheese
            butter
            jelly
            milk
            juice
            candy canes
PM   put ornaments on tree

Friday:
AM   fix the faucet in 4B
       check the hinge and lock on 5A

PM   sweep foyer/stairs
       set up table and chairs

Jack's thoughts were consumed with his annual party, but this year there was more rattling around in his brain. Gloom and doom seemed to permeate the walls of his building.

Come on Jack, think, think…Those Santas on the corner gather there every day. What if…? Would it be worth the risk?

I never want to go back. A juvenile detention center is one thing, but as an adult, where would they put me? I can't allow myself to get caught.

Would it be worth the price if I did?

CHAPTER FOURTEEN

J ack, having nodded off on the sofa, woke up disoriented. It was 11:00 p.m. already, way past his bedtime. He knew he wouldn't be able to fall back asleep without doing his usual bottom-to-top routine check on the building.

There was an inside door from his apartment to the lobby. First, he checked to make sure that the front door was locked before proceeding up the stairs. *Crash!* It was like the sound of a tower of glass resounded down to the lobby. Jack bolted up to the second floor like lightening.

Clutching the keys that were always fastened on his belt loop, he did a 360 on the second floor landing. *Which door?* He stopped to listen.

There was definitely sobbing coming from 2A, Tillie's place. He knocked. No response. He rang the bell. No response. He couldn't wait any longer and unlocked the door.

There was Tillie, sitting back on her knees in the middle of the floor, surrounded by thousands of broken pieces of Rosenthal china. She held a fractured tea cup in her right hand, while her left hand held her forehead. Tears flowed, and rhythmic moaning continued. It appeared that every piece of her delicate chinaware had been broken. Jack looked over to the corner cabinet where it had been kept. The door was wide open, and it seemed that the glass shelf that had held the precious Rosenthal dishes had collapsed, causing this avalanche. The hinges must have loosened over the years.

Jack knew how dear this set of China had been to Tillie. The Bauers had purchased this set in Germany when they married many years ago. Karl was gone, and now those precious pieces would also no longer be there.

"Don't touch the glass, Tillie."

She didn't even look up but continued to sob. Jack walked closer and tried to reach her without crushing more of the china. He managed to go around the coffee table where just a few days ago they sat together, having a tea party with Jasmine and Joey. As he gently rubbed her back he murmured in a low-tone voice, "You're going to be OK."

Finally, she looked up. "Oh, Jack, you can fix many things, but you can't fix this."

He would have done anything to take away her sorrow, but there didn't seem to be any words that would comfort her right now.

"I'll clean it up for you."

Her legs were stiff, and her spirit was broken. It was difficult getting her to her feet. Jack, being strong, was able to put his two arms under hers and practically lift her up. Carefully, he walked her over to the nearby armchair and got her comfortably seated.

"Just sit there and rest, Tillie." Jack walked over to the kitchen sink, got her a glass of water, and placed it in her hands. "Here, Tillie. Take a sip. I'm going downstairs to get the shop vacuum to clean up."

She gave a slight nod. It was as if any inner strength she had was sucked out like a deflated balloon.

As Jack left the apartment, Bob in 2B opened his door. "What happened? Is Tillie all right?"

"Physically, yes. A shelf broke, and lots of her good china shattered. She's mighty upset. I'm going downstairs to get and a dustpan, broom, and my shop vac to clean up."

"What the matter, Daddy? I heard a big noise and got scared." Little Abby, holding on to her daddy's leg, peaked out into the hallway.

"It's OK, little one. Something broke in Mrs. Bauer's apartment, but she's fine."

Jack, always sensitive to the needs of others, wanted to lessen the fright.

"Are you ready for Santa?" Jack asked.

"Yes, Mr. L."

"Did you tell him what you'd like?"

"Yes, look at the note I taped on the door. I wanted to make sure he'll know what to bring me."

Jack took his glasses out of his pocket and carefully read the penciled note.

"So, you want an American Girl doll. Well, I'll tell Santa to be sure to look at your note when I see him."

"Thanks, Mr. L."

"You better go back to sleep because Santa is watching, and I better get that mess cleaned up for Mrs. Bauer."

She let go of her daddy's leg, held her little hand up high, flapped her fingers, and headed back to bed.

"You OK, Jack?"

"Yeah, everything's going to be all right."

Before closing the door, Bob just stood there with a wrinkled brow as he watched Jack hustle downstairs.

By the time the cleanup was completed, Tillie, exhausted from the ordeal, was anxious to retire to her bed. Jack locked up and toted the heavy-duty black garbage bag and shop vac down to the garage. *This time of year, sacks should be filled with presents, not frag-ments of teas gone by.*

Finally settled in his own inner sanctum, Jack tried to relax. He reached for the snow globe, held it tenderly before shaking it. Then he turned it over and wound it. He watched as the flakes once again found their resting spots and listened intently to "Jingle Bells." He was deep in thought. *I know that things don't always turn out as we hope. You always told me, Dad, to do my very best. Well, I'm try-ing. I've got to do this for them. I've thought and thought, and this is the only way I can figure out to do it—maybe not your way.* As the music box within the globe played its dying notes, he carefully returned it to its resting spot. Jack knew the risk he'd be taking. *Sometimes life isn't fair.* He had experienced that first hand.

CHAPTER FIFTEEN

S hortly after getting that bike for Christmas, Jack began working at Sonny's Meat Market. He wasn't a slacker. His mom was
desperate for money after Dad died, and Jack was thankful for
the after-school and weekend delivery job. If it wasn't for that
spoiled rotten bully, Jack's life would have been mighty different.
He knew he should have held back his temper, but being stopped
and thrown off his bike en route to a delivery was more than he
could take. His job was essential, and he was determined that this
lowlife wasn't going to make him lose it. Up until that fateful day,
the taunts were merely verbal, but this time it was different.

Just as Jack was about to get going to the next delivery, he could
hear this sarcastic voice chanting "Nice bike, La Falla." In a flash,
he straddled Jack's front tire. Then, by forcefully grabbing the
handlebars, he flipped Jack off the bike. The size and strength of
this bully was alarming. As Jack glanced upward, he came face to
face with this scum-of-the-earth. He could see massive shoulders
bulging under his black leather jacket. If that wasn't enough to
deal with, Jack noticed that two of his back-up flunkies stood only
about five feet behind him.

"Why don't you get a life and leave me alone," Jack shouted, struggling to free himself from this gorilla of a person.

"You think you can scare me, you mama's boy."

A violent punch put Jack's body flat onto the sidewalk; groceries scattered all over the pavement like debris after a storm. That's when Jack went berserk. There was no stopping him this time. He decided to fix this bully once and for all and began to pummel the stupid, arrogant smirk off his bearded face. Once he started, he was like a runaway plow. He pushed; He shoved. Jack's fists were like jackhammers. He couldn't stop until he found himself being torn away from him by a policeman. He trusted that the police would help.

What followed seemed like an endless fall from the top of Devil's Tower in the Black Hills of Wyoming. He went from the back of a police car to front and center of a court- room to a quick verdict to a juvenile detention center in Broom County, New York. Because he didn't have a father, they assumed that he no longer would have the proper guidance. They said it was better for Jack to be turned over to the state rather than fall into more trouble.

The bully's father, of course, stepped right up to the plate protecting his innocent, burly son. The fact that his father was an attorney empowered him to maneuver within the judicial system. He knew the ropes.

Jack's mother, who had trouble handling the loss of his father, sank into an even deeper depression. *How could I have done this to her?* The guilt of losing his cool and letting her down hovered inside him. Without Jack, his mom was really helpless. Her sister Midge, who lived out west, had offered to help. She had lots of room on the farm. He knew it would be good for his mom to be in a different environment. Maybe she'd be able to get a grip on life once again. Peggy and Jimmy needed the care and guidance that Aunt Midge offered.

CHAPTER SIXTEEN

After the shelf collapsed, destroying all Tillie's treasu[
Rosenthal china, Jack had trouble falling asleep. Thoug[
raced up and down, round and round, like a carousel. His mi[
was programmed to set up for that one day at Christmas. He w[
convinced that there was only one way to go, no matter what th[
consequences. After all, the end result would outweigh the risk.

Saturday morning brought with it the excitement that it alway[
had, but this year was different. Jack knew he had to be a good listener; real Santas always are. He was on a mission to find out what
secret wishes dwelled in the hearts and minds of his apartment
house families.

The jolly songs of Christmas muffled the outside street noises
while the smell of coffee and hot chocolate permeated the air. The
aura of Christmas shed a whole new light on the moods of the tenants as they descended the stairs to join in Jack's annual Christmas
breakfast. About half an hour into the breakfast, Jack left to get
Santa. Shortly after, they could hear Santa's bells jingle as he entered the front door. "Ho, ho, ho!" he bellowed.

here, Santa. We weren't sure you'd make it."
me every year, so I'll know what to bring on

ave a seat," said Casey, as he pulled a chair over

uealed in delight, anxious to sit on Santa's
eir wants in his ear while the residents of 649
changed pleasantries, and snapped a few pic-
giggles were contagious and brought smiles

ermined than ever. You could tell by the ques-
dn't you want PlayStation 3, Nintendo, a key-
oll carriage?" He was fueling thoughts to their
nd their expectations. The parents gave a puz-
rs gone by, Jack had always taken the practical ap-
pair of sneakers, a backpack, jeans, a special shirt,

red
hts
nd
as
e

ta, I don't think your sleigh can handle that much
nouted across the lobby. The last thing Joe wanted on
morning was to see tight lips and frowns.
, Santa." agreed Bob, as his head shook in disbelief.
ust winked back and continued giving the little ones high

ey, Santa, what was in that coffee you had this morning?"
nta winked again, ignoring their remarks, and made mental
s of all their hearts' desires.

CHAPTER SEVENTEEN

That stint at the juvenile detention center was implanted in Jack's brain. Since that time, he continued to tread carefully as if walking on eggs. Well, the eggs were about to be broken. Now or never, he thought.

Since the *now* was decided, the *how* was in the works. It seemed too easy but why not? One week left to pull it off.

"Great party, Mr. L. I think the little ones really thought you were Santa."

"That was the plan, Casey." Together, they put away the table and chairs and cleared the crumbs that were left.

"You can bring the coffeemaker into my kitchen. Just put it on the table; I'll clean it later."

Ever since that incident in the storage room, Casey and Jack had come to terms and were actually developing a friendship. "Where do you want me to put the CD player?"

"Just put it on the desk," responded Jack.

As Casey walked into the apartment, he spotted the Santa suit. "Do you want that Santa suit back in the box and stored down in the basement?"

"Nah, just leave it there; it needs a little more airing after being cooped up in that box for almost a year. It makes me feel jolly. I think I'll keep it hanging around for a bit. We can put it away when we take down the tree."

"OK, Jack. Well, I'd better get back upstairs and see what chores Mom has for me."

CHAPTER EIGHTEEN

Sunday morning, Jack woke up earlier than usual. His brain was tumbling ideas like the bingo cage at the community center. Church was always a part of his Sunday ritual. This Sunday he prayed, "Dear Lord, you know that my intention is to help."

On his way home, he picked up the paper. On Sunday, it was always loaded with advertisements. Jack grabbed the yellow pad on his desk, along with his pen. The mental list from Saturday's gathering was now about to be transformed to the written word.

Fifteen apartments, nineteen children sixteen and under, plus the adults added up to forty-seven people. He was "checking it twice" and didn't want to leave anyone out whether they were "naughty or nice."

"Hmm," he muttered out loud as his eyes canvassed the list. About sixty thousand should do it. Of course Jack's bank account didn't amount to much. Up until a year ago, he had sent money out West on a monthly basis to help his mom. Now that she was no longer alive, and his brother and sister had their own lives in other parts of the United States, he was fending solely for himself. The tenants living under his roof had become his family. Sometimes, the desire to do good overpowered the means of achieving his goal.

That bolt of joy that struck him and uplifted his spirits at the young age of fifteen when the unexpected bicycle was delivered at Christmas time was imprinted in his memory bank. Now he was ready to bring about unanticipated joy, no matter what the consequences might be.

The next step was ready to be carried to fruition. For days, he had witnessed the gathering of the Volunteers of America up on the main shopping avenue. Their motto read "Strive to enrich people's lives...everyday miracles." Well, that was Jack's motto, too.

He eyed the Santa suit that hung on the door frame. *Who could distinguish one Santa from another?* The Con Edison crew was still working on that busy street. They had been there for weeks. It was the same old, same old.

Around ten o'clock would be fine. By then, the apartment building would be emptied out, kids off to school, adults already working at their respective jobs. He couldn't wait any longer. His inner tension was mounting like a volcano getting ready to erupt. The decision was made. Monday morning would be his D-Day.

As Jack once again picked up that glass snow globe, he felt not only soothed but energized as well. Mentally, he wrote out a step-by-step procedure for himself. He'd fold the red suit into a black garbage bag. Leave about 9:45 a.m. and walk down the block and around the corner. The Porta Potty rental for the construction guys would work. It was so close, so easy. No matter what you do, "Give it your personal best," his dad would say.

I'll have to word it just right so no one gets hurt. Tellers never have that much cash. They'd have to ask the manager or head teller. Might as well address the chief.

All the pieces of the plan had to be well thought out, no glitches. Jack sat at his desk with pad and pen and began. He struggled with the words. The message had to be concise and clear.

"Damn it." He crumpled the page, threw it, and began again. Clumps of yellow were slowly filling the basket that sat on the floor beside his desk. He stood up and began to pace back and forth from his desk to the kitchen. He opened the fridge, popped a beer, and tried to focus. The clock continued to tick. The shopping list was well on its way. The note was finalized and safely tucked into his Santa pants pocket. All he had to do was call his friend, Ritchie, the bread man. He decided to wait till Monday night to do that. Hopefully by then, he'd have the dough in his hands.

Jack tossed and turned in between segments of sleep. His mind continued to race like a mouse in a maze, twisting every which way, addressing every conceivable obstacle that might come into play.

CHAPTER NINETEEN

Jack woke up early as usual, listened to the forecast, and peered outside his bedroom window. Light snow was predicted. *Good sign.*

Jack was up before the alarm. He showered and dressed in his usual work clothes, along with his black boots. He then made his normal breakfast, a bowl of cereal and coffee. Morning rounds and chores had to be completed by 9:00 a.m. He needed to adhere to his planned time schedule.

Promptly at 9:45, with garbage bag in hand, he left the building. He walked down the block, careful not to step on a crack while whistling "Jingle Bells" just like he did when he was a kid. His spirits were up, and his gait exhibited a happy-go-lucky attitude. "Here I go," he muttered under his breath as he turned the corner. *Yup, there they are, working away, oblivious to the people walking to and fro.*

He ducked into the Porta Potty, transformed himself, and emerged as a newcomer to the Volunteers of America in his red and white suit. Carefully, he crossed the street and entered the glass doors of the bank, greeting people along the way with a jolly

"Merry Christmas." He stood for a moment to case the lobby. Yup, the manager was at her desk. It wasn't crowded—too early in the day. As he walked over to her desk, he noticed some family pictures with young children. *Good, she'll understand.*

"Good morning, Santa. What can I do for you today?" Without speaking, Jack took off his gloves, reached into his left pants pocket, and handed her the note. Then he put his gloves back on, sat at the edge of the chair, and leaned forward with his forearms resting on the edge of her desk. His deep blue eyes focused on her hands as she slowly unfolded the yellow piece of pad paper. There was a wedding band on her left hand. *She won't take any chances.* She looked up at him with a dazed expression as if she had been hit on the head with a sledgehammer. "Is this a joke?"

The manager watched attentively for his response. His head turned from side to side. It was a clear *no,* and the jolly look that he had had walking into the bank had taken a backward turn. Tucked into his right sleeve, deliberately directed at her, was the edge of the barrel of the black pistol. He adjusted his pose and sat back in the chair. Her face froze. He leaned forward once again and pointed to the words "Please follow my instructions so no one will get hurt." She glanced down, reread slowly, "I only need $60,000, no more, no less," and then looked up at him with a puzzled look. Santa shook his head in agreement. The note specified "No alerts until after I leave. Let us all have a merry Christmas." After sitting rigid for a few seconds, she tilted her head toward him and whispered, "I'll get it."

Jack watched her put her hands on the arms of her black leather chair, swivel around slowly toward the back of the bank, raise herself up, and walk toward the vault. She could feel his intense stare follow her maneuver toward the rear. Every person at the bank was in jeopardy, and she was the person in charge. *Give him whatever he wants,* she thought, *and then the police will take over. Too many lives are at stake.*

The minutes seemed like hours as Jack waited and watched. He tucked the gun back into the red sleeve of his suit, wondering if others could hear the thumping of his heart. Beads of sweat began to form across his brow. He wiped them away with his gloved hand, trying to remain cool, calm, and collected. *What's taking her so long?* No hint of alarm was visible from where he sat. He watched intently until finally, she emerged holding two large, stuffed, brown mailing envelopes. "Here it is, Santa," she uttered, with a soft quiver in her voice. Jack opened the black plastic bag that contained his work clothes, deposited the two envelopes along with the note he had given her, pulled the red plastic tie closed, secured the pistol carefully up his sleeve, stood up, nodded, and exited as quickly as possible, trying not to draw any attention.

He was sure the alarm button would be pressed as soon as he passed through the glass doors if not sooner.

And laying his finger aside of his nose
And giving a nod, up the chimney he rose.

Yeah, wouldn't that be great? Get real, La Falla. He talked to himself as he scurried away like a rat with a big, fat slice of cheese.

CHAPTER TWENTY

His steps quickened as he mingled among the sidewalk shoppers, the workmen, the approaching garbage truck, and the Volunteers of America Santas who still lingered on the sidewalk before heading to their designated posts.

"Damn it," he muttered as he struggled to free himself from the broken piece of wire mesh that stuck out of the overflowing city garbage can. What a klutz! Better to tear the pocket of the red suit than the black garbage bag that he had slung over his shoulder.

Just as Jack ducked into the nearby subway, he heard the police sirens. Quickly, he took his MetroCard out of his pants pocket, swiped it, and headed to the downtown platform. Being familiar with the location of the men's room, he entered and locked it. First, he removed his gloves, along with the black plastic pistol, and fidgeted with the snaps that held the red jacket closed. His hands trembled. Finally, he was able to remove his entire suit of deception. Jack tried to relax his breathing. He squatted down on the john, attempting to gain composure. *Was the sixty K really there?*

He reached into the black garbage bag, pulled out one of the two envelopes, and peered inside. There it was—bundles of one hundred dollar bills. He fanned through a few packs. *Yes—I did it. So far, so good.*

With a hasty clothing switch, he headed back out to the platform and waited anxiously for the next train. Five minutes seemed like five days. He scanned the subway cars as the train pulled in to the station. *Not too crowded.* He was anxious to enter and get out of there. The doors opened. With his winter wool cap and wool gloves back on, he got in and stood holding on to the pole near the door. One stop downtown would get him far enough away yet close enough to walk back home.

He got off as inconspicuously as possible, walked up to the street level, and traversed the ten blocks to get back home. Wearing his usual work clothes and warm jacket, he clenched the tied end of the black garbage bag like the rope of a life raft. The risk was worth it. He yearned to be the unexpected savior and gift giver to those fifteen families. At a young age, Jack had learned that in giving, we receive. The only snag here was the means he chose to be the giver.

The police cars had surrounded the crime scene by the time Detective Pivin pulled up in his black Marquis. He parked behind the police car, and before venturing out into the cold, he put on his earmuffs and buttoned up his black wool overcoat. The wind was blowing, and the snowflakes continued to circle the air.

"Damn, it's cold out here. What happened?" he asked the officer standing outside the door of the bank. Pivin removed his earmuffs to hear the response.

"Santa robbed the bank and walked out with sixty K."

Just then, another police car pulled up with sirens blasting, and Pivin looked around and put his muffs back on. "I hate that sound."

After canvassing the street, he walked into the bank and asked to speak to the manager. "Hello, I'm Detective Pivin. Before you tell me what happened, was anyone hurt?"

"No," she replied, a bit shaken by the whole ordeal.

"OK, now I want you to tell me exactly what happened."

As she told what had transpired, he took out his notepad and recorded the details.

"Interesting, a bank robber who demands a specific amount. Where's the note he handed to you?"

"He must have taken it. I saw the pistol in his right sleeve. He had the barrel pointing directly at me. I didn't want anyone to get hurt, so I just did exactly what was asked."

"Smart move," Pivin commented. "So, only sixty thousand dollars? Not too greedy."

"Yes, Detective. Usually they ask for a lot more, don't they?"

"Must be a recession." He was hoping to ease the tension in her face. She managed a hint of a smile. "So tell me, what did he look like?"

"Santa—red jacket, pants, and hat, all trimmed with white fur."

"Was he wearing glasses?"

"No, but he was wearing gloves."

"Who saw what? Anyone see the getaway sleigh?"

At that point, you could tell the rigidity was waning. Pivin had a unique way of interrogating. He had been on the force for many years. "If you break the law, I'm gonna get you" had always been his attitude; he was successful at his job. Once he had examined the evidence and asked all the questions of the persons involved, he tended to hunt for the less obvious.

Pivin was close to retirement but couldn't imagine what he'd do with his life if he wasn't doing what he liked best. The intrigue of detective work kept his mind occupied. He had been divorced for more than twenty years, had no children, and loved watching the Yankees. Basically, he was a loner.

"Get me a copy of the surveillance tape."

She lifted the phone and called bank security to get it for him. "I'll be back in a little bit; I'm just going to snoop around."

Pivin walked outside and sniffed like a hound dog, looking for clues. His ulcers were acting up again, so he took out his new pack of Rolaids. "Don't litter" had been ingrained in his brain. As he walked toward the end of the block to throw out the wrapper in the city trash can, he spotted a red piece of cloth hanging from the jagged edge of the can's broken mesh. Carefully, he dislodged it. As he did so, his right leather glove, which was carefully tucked under his left arm, accidentally dropped near the curb. He bent down to pick it up and spotted a beaten-up, old, black leather wallet lying on the street side leaning next to the curb. *Wonder how long that's been there?* Being the detective that he was, he took out his handkerchief, discreetly picked it up, and placed it in his right outside overcoat pocket. Later, he would examine it. Right now he had to stay focused on the robbery.

CHAPTER TWENTY-ONE

Jack managed to make it home without bumping into anyone he knew. He opened the side door to his apartment, threw his Santa sack in the corner of the kitchen, and made a mad dash for the bathroom. He collapsed on his knees in front of the toilet and heaved. In between each wave of nausea, he prayed that he could pull this whole thing off. After all, it wasn't for himself. There was too much misery in this world. He prayed for understanding. Maybe someday he could pay it all back.

Finally, after his stomach emptied, Jack was able to attain a bit of composure. He sat back on his calves, put down the lid of the toilet seat, and rested his head on folded forearms until the shaking subsided. Praying for strength, he struggled to stand. He hung on to the sides of the sink and steadied himself before turning on the cold water faucet and splashing his face. He knew he had to get back into the groove of his Monday afternoon routine ASAP.

Slowly, Jack maneuvered toward the kitchen while holding on to the walls as if he was sailing on rough seas. Water—he needed a sip badly. His throat was parched, and he felt as if he had a fever.

He ran the cold water and grabbed the nearby jelly jar glass that he always left on the counter to the right of the sink. He filled it and sipped slowly, as if he had run a marathon. A half-full cup of his morning coffee stood in the sink. *Did I really pull this off?* His breathing rate increased. *Slow and steady. Come on, Jack. Deep breaths.* He glanced over at the black plastic bag that lay there on the yellow linoleum kitchen floor and decided to dump out its contents. Only minutes ago, it was slung over his shoulder. Once again, he tried to slow down his breathing. *Think calm, deep breaths, get control.* Slowly, he began to focus. *Priorities.* I'll need the suit for Saturday morning—the grand finale. *Think, Jack, think.*

He walked to the closet in his bedroom to procure a hanger with clips for the red pull-on fleece pants. Carefully, he shook out the pants and hung them up. The light snow had seeped into the soft fleece and needed to dry. He positioned the jacket over the pants and tucked the hat into the right sleeve. The moustache and beard, which only a short time ago had dressed his visage, were carefully rolled and stuffed into the other sleeve. He reached up and hooked the hanger on the kitchen doorframe, the warmest spot in his apartment. It would certainly be dry by Saturday. Anxious to get that gun out of sight, he rolled it up in the black bag and stuck it in his kitchen trash, which was in the cabinet under the sink. He hated guns, even the fake ones. Jack left the best for last. Carefully, he picked up the two brown envelopes, caressed them as if holding a baby, and kissed them before tossing them into the freezer. He'd count later.

Jack glanced at his to-do calendar, which was tacked on the wall above his kitchen table. Yes, today is still Monday—recyclables needed to be placed in the blue can, newspapers and cardboard had to be bundled or placed in clear plastic bags, NYC rules needed to be followed. He didn't want to be fined. Tuesdays and Fridays were trash pickup days. He knew what he had to do but didn't have the energy to get it done; he felt like a deflated balloon.

For the moment, Jack was glad to be behind closed doors, but he was well aware of the possible consequences of his actions. The clock kept ticking, and he had to go forth.

Surely Tillie would notice if he skipped his routine chores. Looking out the window that faced the front sidewalk was her favorite spot. She knew the comings and goings of the people in 649. Watching helped to pass the time for her. Jack gave Tillie the high sign as he took out the cans.

CHAPTER TWENTY-TWO

Pivin headed back to his car with the swatch of fabric and the wallet carefully tucked away. He had the reputation of being a heist breaker. But who the heist taker behind that red suit was still remained to be seen.

Before driving back to his office, Pivin pulled out a small recording device from the glove compartment of his car. He often used it to get his immediate thoughts on tape. Later on, he would review it and document it on paper.

That evening, he followed his usual routine. After removing his jacket, shirt, and tie, he went to his fridge and popped a cold one. Then he sat down on his comfy, worn-out sofa and flipped through the news channels. Local news was his best bet. Sure enough, there it was: "Santa robbed a bank today, but this one's an imposter. The police and detectives are viewing the surveillance tapes and questioning anyone who saw him. The description is one that we all know so well. No one was hurt. As of this moment, the sixty-thousand-dollar Santa remains elusive. Anyone with information about this incident is asked to call Crime Stoppers at 800-244-TIPS."

Why a specific amount?

Pivin went to his overcoat pocket to remove the small piece of red fleece that he had carefully placed there. He went back to the sofa and sat there, rubbing the fabric between the fingers of his right hand. In his left, he clutched the worn-out black leather wallet he had found. He needed to check out the owner. He placed the cloth scrap on the end table and opened the wallet. Encased in yellowed plastic was a driver's license that read "Jack La Falla." *Hmmm* His thinking cap was on. The address was in the neighborhood. He looked inside and found a ten, two fives, and three singles.

Pivin was a sleuth. He liked getting into the psyche of an individual and finding out what made people tick. He continued to dig into the wallet and found an insurance card, a scratched-off lottery ticket, a business card for Sonny's Meat Market, and a Saint Jude prayer card. *What if...?*

His constant analysis was like a revolving door. Sometimes he rotated a few times before deciding if he wanted in or out. Check the details—the obvious and the not so obvious. For Pivin, a hunch was like a piece of cheese for a mouse.

Think I'll check out this Jack La Falla tomorrow.

CHAPTER TWENTY-THREE

J ack's stomach was still unsettled after he completed the day's chores. He knew his body required nourishment. A can of soup with a side of saltines would do the trick. *Relax, relax.* He paced back and forth in his tiny railroad apartment. While the soup was heating in the microwave, he walked through the living room to his bedroom. There on the desk was the snow globe. "Help me," he unconsciously cried out in a desperate plea as he reached out, clasped the coolness of the glass with both hands, and held it close to his chest. He had taken a gamble. He wished he could shake off those worries with one shake, but the real world didn't work that way. *What will happen?*

Jack's curiosity kept nagging. He couldn't keep still. Finally, he placed the globe in its resting spot and set up a snack tray in the usual spot in his living room. He got the saltines along with a cup of soup, and set them down carefully. *Courage, courage.* He flipped on the TV to the local news channel. The meteorologist was predicting more cold weather with a chance of snow for tomorrow, clear and cold for the rest of the week, maybe a chance of light snow on Christmas Day. "Stay tuned for the details of a local bank robbery. Looks like Santa was short of cash."

Beads of sweat sprung up on Jack's brow like the remnants of a spring shower. His eyes remained glued to the screen. The commercials seemed endless. *Come on, come on.* Jack could once again feel his heart beat accelerate. He held the cup of soup up to his lips but was unable to sip. His empty stomach began to do flip-flops.

"We'll look at some of the stories for the next half hour right after the break." *Another commercial.* With trembling hands, Jack set the cup back down on the snack table and waited. Deep breaths didn't seem to help.

"And now back to the news. At about ten thirty this morning, at a small, local branch of Citibank, Santa walked away with sixty thousand dollars. The surveillance tape shows a person in a red and white Santa suit, approximately five feet ten inches tall, a bit stocky, with a white beard and moustache and black, laced-up, leather work boots, carrying a black plastic garbage bag. The note that he handed to the manager demanded sixty thousand dollars in large bills. Fortunately, no one was hurt. As of right now, the identity of this Santa remains unknown. Anyone with information about this incident is asked to call Crime Stoppers at 800-244-TIPS."

Maybe, just maybe. Jack began to feel a bit of relief. His breathing finally slowed and so did his heart rate. He took a handkerchief out of his pocket and wiped his brow. Slowly, he managed to sip his soup and munch on a few saltines while the rest of the news played on. Feeling a bit more settled, he decided to check out the loot. He walked to the freezer and took out the two envelopes. Jack dumped the contents. Sixty bundles of one-hundred-dollar bills landed like a colossal collision of miniature sleds and decorated the Formica surface of Jack's kitchen table. Santa had succeeded. Wishes could now become realities. These stacks of bills held the means to ear-to-ear grins and joyous jumps on Christmas morning. Everyone needs a Santa at some point in their lives, and Jack decided this one day at Christmas would be it.

Tomorrow I'll call Richie, the bread man, to see if I can borrow his truck on Thursday after he finishes his route.

Jack showered and got ready for bed. He felt as if he had been through the ringer of an old washing machine. He took out the shopping list he had started on Sunday. *Better check it twice.* Jack certainly didn't want to forget anyone in the building, no matter what his or her age might be. His rough figure of sixty K had to cover it all.

Sleep did not come easily that night. Jack twisted and turned like a balled-up piece of yarn. Too many things were running through his brain, and of course the possibility of getting caught continued to linger. He tried to push that aside and catch a few winks before 5:30 a.m. arrived.

Jack jolted upright in bed to the obnoxious sound of a piercing buzz. *Where am I? Are the guards conducting a fire drill?* He flipped on the lamp and looked around. *This is not a cot. Thank God I'm not there.* His tee shirt and pillowcase were wet. He must have been sweating profusely. His hands were still clammy. Finally, he got up and walked over to the desk to silence the buzz. He purposely never kept the alarm next to his bed for fear of oversleeping.

Jack sat back down on his bed and tried to sort out some meaning. It seemed so real. He was back at the juvenile detention center, trying to fall asleep on his cot. There was a Christmas tree in the dorm. He could see Santa wheeling in a bike, his bike. Jack watched as Santa flicked down the kickstand with his foot before turning to look at Jack. Then Santa reached into his sack and pulled out a snow globe. While holding the wooden base of the globe, Santa extended his arm toward Jack. There was no figure of Santa inside, no sack of toys. As Jack squinted his eyes in the hopes of trying to see clearly, Santa extended his arm pushing the globe nearer to Jack's face. It was then that he saw his father's deep-set, dark brown eyes and furrowed brow glaring back at him right through the glass of the globe. The last thing Jack remembered before waking was Santa shrugging his shoulders. *Now what?*

CHAPTER TWENTY-FOUR

Pivin woke up at 6:00 a.m., fifteen minutes before the regularly scheduled alarm. He was anxious to get a handle on this Jack La Falla character. As always, coffee was first on his list. Pivin needed that caffeine fix before heading to the shower. The coffeemaker was the only appliance on his kitchen counter. He opened the small, white, apartment-size refrigerator, took out the red can of Folgers, and opened it. Only one scoop left. *Darn it.* He made a mental note to pick up some at the first grocery store he passed that day. With a busy schedule ahead of him, he needed his caffeine fix. One scoop in a six-cup pot wasn't going to do it. Hoping to find a hidden can of coffee, he stooped over, stuck his head into the refrigerator, and proceeded to shuffle through a few of the week's leftover take-out containers that lingered on the middle shelf. In the back right corner, he noticed the next best thing, a can of Coke. He grabbed it, popped it open, and waited for the fizz to settle before taking a sip. Any form of caffeine would help give him his much-needed kick-start to a new day.

With Coke in hand, he meandered into the living room and picked up the beat-up wallet that he had left on the coffee table.

The wheels inside his head slowly began to spin. He called the precinct to tell them that he had some more investigating to do regarding yesterday's bank robbery. As a police detective, his job was to collect evidence and gather information about criminal activity. Pivin was good at what he did, and his job was his life.

His three-room apartment in the Tremont section of the Bronx suited him just fine. It was all the space he needed and convenient for working in the Bronx and NYC area. Pivin lived alone and was seldom there. From every corner of his apartment, he could easily hear the radio alarm on his night table go off at the usual 6:15 a.m. It was set on 880 AM, news and weather every ten minutes. Chance of snow was in the forecast almost every day this week. It didn't surprise Pivin that the Santa bank robbery made the morning news.

After his shower, Pivin wrapped a tattered gray towel around his waist and took out a can of shaving cream and his razor from the medicine cabinet. After a quick shake of the can, he squirted out the shaving cream into the palm of his left hand and spread it around the stubble on his face, which magically appeared every morning. He squinted into the mirror as he mowed off the whiskers. His reflection portrayed a cross between Columbo and Oscar Madison. *Not bad for a fifty-four-year-old.*

Pivin was fortunate to be able to make up his own schedule after having more than thirty years on the force. He was a trusted detective, thorough and successful. He knew he could retire soon but had no intention of doing so because he loved what he did.

Think I'll start the day by driving over to this address and checking out this dude. *Mmm...why? Nah, too easy...but you never know.*

The old black Mercury Marquis sputtered a bit as Pivin turned the key. He had to leave it parked on the street, so sometimes the cold affected its start up. Like its driver, it needed to idle a bit before taking off. Pivin sat quietly while the defroster did its magic. This was his get-into-gear time.

He drove to the corner deli, parked up on the curb, and went in for his daily morning quick stop. Steve saw him coming and poured the usual, a sixteen-ounce cup of black coffee. Pivin placed his two bucks down on the counter as he glanced down to view the day's headlines on the shelf below.

Daily News—Santa…
NY Post—Santa…
Newsday—Santa…

"Did you hear about that Santa robbery?" Steve inquired.

"Yeah, heard it on the morning news. There are so many of those guys around this time of year. Guess I'll go on a Santa hunt today."

"Have a good one."

"You too, buddy."

Pivin got back in his car, put his coffee in the cupholder near the dashboard, pulled out the license of Jack La Falla, studied the photo ID, and placed it on the front seat of his car. The coffee, as usual for this time of year, managed to fog up his window. He wiped the steam from the front windshield with the deli napkins and proceeded slowly through the morning rush hour traffic toward 649 Longwood. It looked like a possible snow sky, cold and cloudy.

Jack's address was only a block and a half from the bank. *Interesting.* Pivin put the wallet back in his overcoat pocket before getting out of the car. He surveyed the building. *No garbage flying around, a wreath on the door, looks fairly decent for this neck of the woods.*

As he walked up to the front door of the apartment house, one of the tenants rushing out practically knocked Pivin over.

"Sorry." He held the door open, expecting Pivin to enter.

"I'm looking for a Jack La Falla. Does he live here?"

"You mean Jack, the super-duper super?"

"Yeah, Jack the super—" Pivin wasn't sure he'd heard the rest correctly and gave that puzzled look.

"Well, that's what we who live here call him. Look at this place. We didn't nickname him the super-duper super for nothing. He makes this dump of a neighborhood look like a mini-Rockefeller Center. Don't see too many other buildings around here that look like this one."

"Yeah." With the door still open, Pivin's eyes scanned the lobby.

"Well, if you want him, professor, you'll probably find him around the side of the building doing the garbage sort."

"Thanks. Have a good day." *Professor—I've never been called that before. Guess it's the black overcoat.*

"Gotta run."

"Thanks."

Pivin walked over to the side of the building and noticed a man around five feet, ten inches with a stocky build.

"Excuse me, Jack?" It was so cold that he could see his breath as he spoke.

"Yeah," Jack responded without looking up, as he tied up the newspapers and cardboard for the next trash pickup.

"Jack, the super?"

"You're looking at him." Jack, always being the polite individual, continued, "How can I help you?" Jack was now brought to attention and stood upright like a wooden soldier.

"Let me introduce myself. My name is Detective Pivin," he responded, as he extended his hand.

Holy shit, Jack thought, *it's not even twenty-four hours, and they got me.* His stomach dropped as if he were riding the Cyclone at Coney Island. He stood there in shock and tried to gather his wits about him. *Deep breaths, deep breaths. Sonny always used to say, "If you want to dance, you have to pay the band." Was this pay-up time?"*

"I'm a bit dirty. Don't think you'd want to touch these." Jack brushed his hands together, quickly trying to act nonchalant.

While gathering his thoughts, he proceeded to pick up and move some of the garbage cans as if they were giant-size chess pieces. He didn't want to be checkmated. "What did you say your name was?" Jack wanted to be sure he'd heard it correctly.

"Detective Pivin," he repeated, while taking out his ID and flipping it open for Jack to see. "You have a place where we can talk? It's real cold out here."

Jack tied up the last bag and slowly headed to the side door of his apartment. *I'm not running. I'm not going anywhere. It just didn't work. OK, but at least I tried. Maybe I went about it the wrong way.* A flashback to the wait in the dentist's office entered his brain. *If you have to pull the tooth, just do it. The anticipation is worse.* "OK, let's go into my apartment."

It was warm and toasty as they entered. "Have a seat, Detective Pivin." Jack motioned to one of the two chairs at the kitchen table. "How can I help you?"

"Thank you." As Pivin sat, he glanced down at Jack's feet. *Yup, beat-up black leather. I'll have those techies at the lab zoom in on the boots.* "Well, I'm hoping that you can help me," Pivin continued. "You see, there have been a series of break-ins in this neighborhood. It seems that more robberies occur around the holidays. I guess people are desperate. Maybe some of these didn't make the headlines, but I was wondering if you saw or heard anything?"

Now Jack felt as if he had stepped off the Cyclone—still a little shaky from the ride, but his stomach wasn't heaving. "No, nothing at the moment. But if I hear anything, I'll be glad to help you out. I'll keep my eyes and ears posted."

As Pivin stood up, he handed Jack his card and then suddenly pointed to the Santa suit that hung on the doorframe behind Jack. "Hey, what are you doing with that outfit?"

Jack couldn't believe he let this guy in his apartment with that hanging in clear view. "Oh, that. Yes, every year I play Santa for the kids in the building. I'll be using it on Christmas morning as I do every year. Thought I'd air it out a bit. I like to bring a little joy into their lives."

"Well, you really ought to sew up that nasty tear in the jacket. Have a nice Christmas, and be sure to call me if you notice anything suspicious."

"Will do, Detective."

Jack collapsed in the chair after Pivin left. *Is this guy just toying with me? He gave me his card. Break-ins in the neighborhood, especially this time of year. Yeah, so?*

Pivin walked back to his car, took a sip of his cold coffee, and then reached into his pocket to pull out the swatch of red fleece fabric and rubbed it between his fingers. *Nice work, Pivin—but why would he do such a thing?*

The wheels were churning in Pivin's head. He always acted cautiously and liked to figure out the psyche of an individual before jumping to conclusions. Detective work was like putting together the pieces of a jigsaw puzzle.

"I like to bring joy to these kids."

Why sixty K?

Should I take Jack in on suspicion?

Red swatch matched jacket.

Has tree in lobby.

No visible signs of fleeing.

He's out there doing his chores.

I'm the only one who knows about the wallet and the swatch of red from the Santa suit Think I'll stake him out for a bit. He doesn't seem to be running away.

CHAPTER TWENTY-FIVE

*L*ots of neighborhood break-ins—really? Leaving the Santa suit out to *dry. The pocket that I didn't even realize was torn. Instructions to call him if I notice anything unusual.* Pivin's words were doing somersaults in his head. Jack took the card and tossed it into the kitchen junk drawer. The detective's sudden appearance puzzled him, but worrying about it wasn't going to get the job done. Jack knew he needed to get his butt into gear.

Beads of sweat trickled down the sides of his cheeks. As he hurried into the bathroom to splash some cold water on his face, he realized that he was still wearing his quilted work jacket. He unzipped it hastily and threw it on the floor. One quick glance into the mirror above the sink reflected his reddened face. *Was it the warmth of the apartment or the fear of getting busted? Deep breaths, deep breaths.* He needed to calm down and think.

Jack picked up his jacket on his way back to the kitchen, poured himself a cold drink of water, sat down at the table, and looked up at the suit, which still hung on the doorframe. *Yeah, maybe I should sew up that rip. I can't believe he noticed that. Well, he is a detective.*

The list was there on the table where he had left it. *Enough of this sitting around.* He put on his jacket and went outside to finish up where he had left off. The sting of cold air and sleet tapped his face like a wake-up call and thankfully cleared his brain. Christmas morn was fast approaching, and he had lots to do over and above his regular Jack the super tasks.

The noon church bells rang. Half the day was already gone. *I better go in and call Ritchie.*

Jack had Richie's cell number, one of his few personal contacts, programmed into his phone. They had been friends since Jack worked at Sonny's.

"Hey, Ritchie, how's it going?

"Busy as hell, Jack. What's up?"

"I need a favor."

"What do you need, buddy?"

"I need to borrow your bread truck on Thursday to pick up a hot water heater for the building."

"Aw, can't you wait till next week? This is busy season."

"Wish I could have planned for the old heater to break after Christmas. Thank goodness there's more than one in the building, but the other one's on shaky ground, too. I can't chance it. If it was in the dead of summer, I wouldn't be so desperate. With the holidays, they won't deliver. That's why I have to pick it up myself."

"OK, you said Thursday. Let's see…today's Tuesday already…let me think how we could do this."

"You know, Rich, I wouldn't ask if I didn't really need it."

"OK. Well, how 'bout you pick it up at six thirty Thursday morning? You know I only get in about five thirty and need some sleep before I start again. Tell you what. I'll leave the key under the mat. The van will be in my driveway, as usual, but you have to promise to have it back to me that same day by five thirty p.m. at the latest, and make sure it's got a full tank of gas. Customers want their bread orders, and I have to get to the bakery to pick up the rolls, bread, Danish, and stuff. You know my routine."

"Thanks so much, Richie. I owe you one, pal."

"We always seem to owe each other one. That's what friends are for."

Phew. Jack sighed as he hung up the phone. He scanned the list he had made. *What will be the toughest to find? Mmm…Rosenthal china.* Tillie was like a grandmother figure to him, since he had never known his own grandparents. Tillie was a giver. She never asked for anything. Losing her china was devastating to her. Maybe he could put a smile on her face when she opened her present. But first, he had to find it, and there wasn't much time.

Jack whipped out his trusty guide, the NYC *Yellow Pages. China— nothing. Rosenthal—nothing, Antiques—maybe. Department store— yeah, that ought to do it.* He went down the alphabetical listings. The first major one was Bloomingdale's on Fifty-Ninth and Lexington. He dialed and got the automated voice system: "Welcome to Bloomingdale's. If you are calling about—" Jack listened to the selections until finally, it said, "Please tell me the name of the department you would like."

"China," Jack responded clearly into the phone.

"Please hold."

Jack waited. The phone rang, and surprisingly, a real person picked up. Jack was impressed at how well their system worked. "Do you carry Rosenthal china?"

"Yes, we do. We carry a variety of styles. Do you know the name of the pattern?"

"No, I don't, but I'm sure I'll know it when I see it. Thank you."

Great! I can take the subway and pick that up tomorrow. He put a check mark next to Tillie's name. *Let's see who else I can take care of tomorrow while I'm downtown. Yeah, the girls, Jasmine and Abby. I heard them talking about American Girl dolls, whatever they are. Let me look them up and see where they're located.* Jack thumbed through the yellow pages again to find American Girl stores. Fifth Avenue and Forty-Ninth Street would be an easy walk from Bloomingdales on Fifty-Ninth.

The rest would be easy. *Paramus New Jersey has great shopping, and it's not too far. Richie's step van will be perfect.*

CHAPTER TWENTY-SIX

Pivin had a few more questions for the bank manager, as well as the others employees who had been there on Monday morning. He also needed to review the surveillance tape, which had been collected yesterday. Investigators like Pivin were turning more and more to footage for helpful glimpses of the crime. It was important to scrutinize those minutes from Monday morning for some clues other than a red and white Santa outfit. Computer wizardry often enabled the techies to zoom in and get a closer look. Fuzzy blobs could sometimes be converted into clearer images. Of course the white beard, moustache, hat, and the rest of the outfit made it difficult to identify the person underneath it all. "Can you zoom in on the boots for me? That might be another clue."

"Let's see what we can do."

Pivin waited while they played around with the video tape. "The surveillance camera just caught the heel of the boot. Looks like Timberland to me."

"Thanks for the info. Knowing the kind of boot might be helpful." Pivin noted it on the pocket pad of information that he carried near and dear to his heart.

Next, he decided to pick up a cup of tea with lemon to ease his scratchy throat and stuffy nose. He needed to establish a clear-cut scenario of the crime that took place. Pivin's special assignment was burglary, and he was noted for putting together the bits and pieces of information. The first responding officer to the scene had debriefed Pivin in step-by-step order. One thing was evident; the witnesses were not involved in the robbery.

For the time being, Pivin was holding on to the swatch and wallet. He wasn't ready to reveal any of that as evidence. After all, none of it was found at the crime scene. Pivin's eagle eyes just happened to spot the fabric on the trash can near the corner as he walked the street and then the wallet, which lay on the street next to the curb. *Coincidence? Maybe.*

Having the license made it easy to do a background check. Pivin was used to doing those type of investigative searches. He had to get back to the precinct for that as well as to write up the report. The media was having a field day with this one. He had to document the known facts accurately. *What was the real story behind this robbery?*

Pivin liked to get into a person's psyche and see what made him or her tick. As a pastime, he liked to read some of Sigmund Freud's works, as well as Carl Jung's. Pivin enjoyed figuring out the instinctual drives of an individual as well as his or her personality. Jack would be his next study.

He'd begin staking out this La Falla dude on Wednesday. Apartment house superintendents began their days early, so, he'd try to get there at 6:00 a.m. For the next several days, Pivin thought he would just hang out in his car across the street from the building and observe.

CHAPTER TWENY-SEVEN

Late Tuesday night, Jack took out one of the envelopes of money from the freezer stash to cover the cost of Tillie's china and the two American Girl dolls that he planned on picking up for Jasmine and little Abby. He withdrew two thousand and returned the rest for tomorrow night's final withdrawal. That should be more than enough for not only the china and the dolls but maybe even a gift certificate for the American Girl store. The image of his little sister dressing up her baby doll and carrying it around the apartment like it was a real baby flashed into his head. He hadn't thought about her in years and never even heard from her anymore. His family had become the renters who lived in 649. *Yeah, I'll get them each a gift certificate.* Then they'd be able to pick out an outfit for their dolls and maybe a matching one for themselves. The jolly bug was biting again. He prayed that he'd be able to pull it off.

Jack scanned the list. Every apartment number was there, and under each one were the occupants. Before going to sleep, he double-checked to make certain everyone would get something they had whispered in Santa's ear or something that was beyond their wildest dreams.

Jack got up early as usual. Tillie had called at 7:00 a.m. to tell him that the overhead light in her bathroom wasn't working. He needed to take care of that first and then do his regular maintenance before heading downtown. Tillie was the house watchwoman. She knew the routines.

After breakfast he headed upstairs and knocked on Tillie's door. She was waiting.

"Glad you're here, Jack. It's so dark in there without that light. I had to use my flashlight early this morning before I called you."

"Thank goodness I gave you one of those to keep handy. Never know when it'll be needed. I wouldn't want you to trip or bump into something in the wee hours of the morning."

Jack took the step stool, unscrewed the fixture, and changed the bulb. "Hey, Tillie, look." Jack waited for Tillie to turn in his direction before flipping the wall switch. "Let there be light."

"Wunderbar!" Tillie applauded and cracked a big smile. It didn't take much to make her happy.

"Hey, Jack, you better come look. There's a guy sitting in a big, black car across the street. I don't recognize the car. I don't think he's a regular. He's been sitting there since I got up this morning. He doesn't seem to be moving. Maybe he's frozen." Tillie stood up and headed toward the kitchen. "Want a cup of coffee?"

Jack put away the step stool and went to look while Tillie tottered into the kitchen to pour his coffee. A freshly brewed cup of coffee was always the payback.

"Let me see. Guess he's OK, Tillie. I see a big black car pulling out."

"Good."

"I'll take that cup of coffee now, Miss Nosey Pants."

"Oh, Jack," she snickered. "You know you have to be careful. You never know who's out there. Someone has to watch out and see what's going on in the neighborhood."

She should only know, thought Jack. He liked keeping her safe and happy.

It was ten o'clock already. *I better get cleaned up a bit and get downtown, shop, and return before the evening rush.*

He didn't like carrying too much money in his wallet on the subway, so he'd spread it out in front and inside pockets as well as his socks. It wasn't often that he had a lot of "coupons," as he liked calling those greenbacks.

Jack changed before loading the loot. *Where's my MetroCard and wallet?* He knew he had it on Monday and began to retrace his steps. *I used the card to catch the subway. It must be in the jacket pocket.* The red fleece was still hanging on the doorframe. "Yep, here it is, but where is my wallet?" He noticed the tear that Pivin had pointed out. "Maybe I put it in my pants pocket." He was talking out loud to himself, as he often did. He checked the fleece pants, no pockets in those. Next, he pulled out his work pants and checked. No luck. "When did I use it last?"

Maybe it was in the black plastic bag. He pulled the bag out of the trash, unrolled it, and shook out its contents—only one plastic gun bounced out. He turned the bag inside out. Nothing. *Think, Jack, think...*

Getting panicky would do him no good. *Deep breaths, deep breaths.* He really didn't need his wallet until tomorrow when he picked up Richie's step van. His license was in it. "OK, I'll look for it when I get back. It's gotta be here somewhere."

CHAPTER TWENTY-EIGHT

Jack had never crossed the threshold of Bloomingdales and felt a bit warm around the collar. He zipped open his Sunday jacket, took off his wool hat and gloves, and shoved them into his pockets as he looked around. It was a wonderland of decorations, and he had thought his lobby looked great. He meandered his way through the cosmetics and perfume counters toward the elevators. It took him a while to scan the index for each floor. Finally, he located china, got into the elevator, pressed the button, and ascended. As the doors opened on his floor, he got out and just stood there mesmerized, looking left and right. He was definitely in unknown territory. People were shuffling all around him. Jack froze. Only his eyes were moving back and forth like the pendulum of a clock. Finally, he spotted a salesperson and got up the courage to head her way. "Rosenthal, please," he requested.

"Right over here, sir. Just follow me."

Jack was definitely out of his element. His eyes were drawn to a pattern that looked similar to Tillie's floral print. "I'll take four of these place settings, please."

"Let me see if we have them in stock."

"Thank you." He took out his handkerchief and wiped away the beads of sweat on his brow while he stood and waited.

"Looks like you're in luck. I'll have them brought up to the cashier's desk right over there." She pointed him in the right direction. "Is there anything else you'd like?"

"Could you gift wrap them for me?"

"Certainly. What type of gift card would you like? Is it a for a wedding?"

"Oh no, just Christmas."

Jack paced as if he were in the waiting room of a maternity ward until she finally returned with the four place settings in one big box. Jack's eyes widened with delight. *Yes, I did it.*

"OK, sir, let's see. Four place settings, plus the tax and gift wrap comes to a total of nine hundred fifty-one dollars and seventy-seven cents. "How would you like to pay for that, sir?"

"Cash."

"Cash?" she questioned.

"Yes, cash." he said, nodding. How difficult was that to understand? Jack had carefully tucked five hundred dollars in four locations. He reached into his left inside coat pocket and his right front pants pocket and handed her the ten one-hundred dollar bills.

She counted and gave him the change, which he pushed down deep into his right front pants pocket. Then he picked up the shopping bag laden with the beautifully wrapped package, thanked the saleslady once again, headed back to the elevator, and retraced his steps to the outside. His heart jumped for joy as he exited and walked up Fifth Avenue. Holiday music seemed to be everywhere intermingled with bell ringers. This Santa had no time to waste. American Girls dolls were next.

The sidewalks were crowded, and Jack was thankful it wasn't snowing. He walked to the main entrance on Fifth only to find that he had to wait on line to get inside. The china was getting heavy, and he rested it carefully on the sidewalk next to the show-case window as he inched his way forward. Luckily, it was double bagged. It was like waiting to buy a movie ticket on a Saturday night, which he seldom did. But this line moved at a snail's pace. Jack was astonished by the window displays. *Wait on line to buy a doll? What am I, crazy? A whole department store dedicated to dolls?* He needed to be patient if he wanted to succeed. The outfits on these showcase dolls were far, far better than the clothes on the people he knew.

Jack had never heard of this special type of doll until Jasmine whispered it into his ear at the Christmas breakfast. He was deter-mined more than ever to make wishes realities. If Jasmine had a doll, little Abby would surely want one too.

Jack was to find out quickly that this was no ordinary store. Finally, after a thirty-minute wait, he was welcomed inside. Doll clothes displays were everywhere, shelves and shelves of choices. He went with the flow of the hordes of people, mostly women and little girls who led him left and then right toward the escalator. There he stood rigid and read the list of items on each of the three floors. A hair salon was on the first floor. *You're kidding. I definitely didn't want to go near there.* With a look of desperation written all over his face, he headed toward the back counters.

"Perhaps I can be of some assistance, sir."

Boy, do I ever need help. I thought Bloomies was over the top.

"Yes," He jumped at the offer. "I need help badly. I'd like to buy two dolls and have no idea of where to begin."

"Before I show you some of them, perhaps you could give me some idea of the ages of the girls."

He was thinking hard. "Well, Jasmine goes to school. I think she's in the first grade. Does that help?"

She nodded with a smile, so Jack continued. "The little one, Abby, is—" He took a step back and put his hand, palm down, at the edge of his jacket. "About this high."

"OK, now can you tell me if they have light or dark hair and possibly the color of their eyes?"

"You're hitting me with tough stuff." Jack was easing up a bit and cracked a smile. "I think the first grader has dark hair and dark eyes. Abby I know has blond curls 'cause I usually give her head a little pat when I see her. How am I doing so far?"

"Great. Now I have an idea of what you might like. I'll bring you a few baby dolls to look at for the little one and other choices for the first grader, along with some outfits to choose from. Stay right here."

"No problem." Jack unzipped his jacket. The pressure he had felt began to release like a blood pressure cuff. Not only was he being helped, he managed a spot at the counter and was able to straddle the shopping bag. He was definitely staying put until she returned.

It was only about ten minutes before she reappeared with an armload of choices, dolls as well as outfits. Jack was pleased. He told the saleslady that they had to be special for these two little ones. They had never had anything like this. She helped Jack make the selections, offered to gift wrap them, and even suggested a gift certificate for accessories and future shopping.

"Wow, that's a great idea!" Jack's eyes twinkled.

"What amount would you like to put on the gift card?

"I dunno—maybe one hundred? How much are these dolls anyway?"

"With the tax, the dolls and outfits come to four hundred thirty-nine dollars. Would you like the gift certificates added on?

A definitive "Yes" was given in reply. No hesitation in Jack's voice.

"And will you be paying by credit card or check?"

"Cash." Jack bent down for a second and casually retrieved the cash from his right sock and the rest from his left front pants pocket. He carefully counted out seven hundred-dollar bills and tucked the remaining three bills back into his sock while waiting for the change. Jack gathered up his stash of presents and headed back to the subway. He was as pleased as a partridge in a pear tree.

Before he took the subway home, Jack carefully placed his packages in two black garbage bags that he had brought with him. Once he was safely in his apartment, he pulled out his desk chair and gingerly placed them on the floor underneath his desk. As he did so, he bellowed "Santa Claus is Coming to Town."

That night, he knew he had to search for his wallet. Methodically, he went through every pocket in the pants he had worn and both of his jackets. He even turned each pocket inside out. He got down on his knees to check under the bed. There was nothing there other than some dust. He lifted the cushions on the sofa in the living room. No luck. *I'll just have to take the copies from the file. Thank goodness I did that for safekeeping.*

CHAPTER TWENTY-NINE

Pivin's Wednesday morning stakeout didn't last too long. His throat was sore, and he felt congested. A cold was definitely brewing. Two hours of sitting in his car became unbearable. *I'm not as young as I used to be. Better head to the drugstore and get some medication and soothing cough drops before it gets worse.* He pulled out and drove to the Rite Aid just down the block.

"Cold medications?" he asked the clerk at the front counter. She directed him to aisle five at the back of the store. As he maneuvered his way he passed the card section, he couldn't help overhearing a small child's jubilant voice rising above the holiday music playing in the store.

"Mommy, Mommy, look at this one. I think Mr. L. would like this card, and it's big enough for everyone to sign."

The "Mr. L." caught Pivin's attention. He stopped and began to peruse some cards. Not that he was planning to send any, but a detective has that natural instinct to stop, look and listen.

The little girl's mother nodded in agreement. "Yes, Abby, I think you might have found the perfect card for Jack."

Pivin's ears perked up like a hunting dog that just picked up the scent of a rabbit.

"Read it, Mommy. Read what it says."

"'To someone special at Christmas.'" Abby's mom opened the card and continued reading out loud. "'May this Christmas be as special as you are. Wishing you peace and joy at Christmas and throughout the new year.' Well, that sounds just fine, don't you think, Abby?"

"Yes, Mommy, let's buy it."

"OK, now we just have to buy some cigars to go with that card. All the tenants in the building want to give him something he enjoys once in a while."

Could it be the same Jack, Mr. L? Coincidence? Pivin, being the sleuth who made him a successful detective, was possibly on a roll once again.

He proceeded to the cough medication section, selected daytime and nighttime congestion aids as well as cough drops, and on his way to the checkout counter found some herbal tea bags with honey. He decided to call it a day and head home. On Thursday, he vowed to make another early attempt to see what Jack might have up his sleeve.

The cold medication seemed to have done its magic because Pivin woke up at five the next morning and was more energetic. He was washed and dressed by five-thirty, stopped for his usual cup of coffee, and drove to Jack's neighborhood. As he turned onto Longwood Avenue, he spotted Jack walking toward Prospect. *Where could he possibly be going at this ungodly hour of the morning?*

Pivin pulled to the side, stopped his car, and watched. *Think I'll keep a distance but follow behind. What is this guy going to pull now?*

CHAPTER THIRTY

B efore leaving his apartment, Jack had stuffed three thousand dollars neatly around each ankle and pulled up his work socks nice and high. The remaining fifty-two thousand plus a bit was divided among the two pockets on the flannel shirt under his sweatshirt, the two inside pockets of his quilted jacket, and the front pockets of his pants. Winter clothes concealed the bulges. He was set to go.

Richie had left the keys under the mat as promised. *It's great having good, reliable friends.* Jack climbed in the driver's seat, made the sign of the cross, and started the engine. "Yeah, baby, let's get on with the show." Jack put the radio on 880 AM to listen to the news and traffic. He headed toward the George Washington Bridge. He knew that Paramus, New Jersey, had a variety of stores in and around a huge shopping plaza. The people in Jack's building certainly wouldn't be shopping in New Jersey. He just had to be cognizant of the time. He had promised Richie that he'd have the truck back to him in time for his bread run. Holiday time was always more demanding than usual. Everyone wanted their delivery at the scheduled time or earlier.

Pivin was on his tail, far enough behind so he wouldn't be obvious. Thankfully, the white step van was an easy spot.

Jack took his time going down Prospect Avenue toward East 164th Street. He knew he had to take the upper level of the George Washington Bridge. Morning traffic was already beginning to build and would double the driving time. He figured it would take him at least one hour. During the last week before Christmas, the big stores like Best Buy and Toys R Us advertised long hours of operation. This time of year, many of the stores opened their door by 8:00 a.m. Best Buy would be his first stop.

Jack slowed at the cloverleaf where Route 4 met Route 17. He would be there soon. The radio was set at 880 AM—news, weather, and traffic. "No new leads in that sixty-thousand-dollar Santa mystery, the investigation continues, and now stay tuned for the traffic and weather." Jack listened intently. His thoughts were focused on Christmas morning. He wanted everything to be perfect. The news continued, "There's a good chance of light snow on Christmas Eve."

For a split second, Jack was inside the snow globe, picturing himself on Christmas morning. "*Yes!*" Jack shouted, as he turned into the parking lot of Best Buy. That would certainly add the perfect setting. He pulled into a spot so that the back of the truck faced the front entrance of the store. Luckily, the lot was still fairly empty. It was only 7:30 a.m., time for a quick breakfast. He locked up the van and traversed the parking lot toward the bagel shop. It was busy with the locals getting their morning pick-ups. Before heading to the counter to order a poppy seed bagel with cream cheese, Jack walked over to the coffee machine, poured himself a medium-size cup of regular coffee, and added milk and one sugar. The aroma of coffee and bagels helped Jack calm the flutter of excitement he felt.

All this time Pivin was parked in the lot awaiting Jack's next move. *I'm quite sure Mr. L. didn't drive over the George Washington Bridge to Paramus for a bagel and coffee. I think New York bagels are better than Jersey bagels, but he's in a bread truck. I guess the bread truck is out of bagels.* Spending lots of time by himself, Pivin often verbalized his inner thoughts. *All this bagel talk is making me hungry.*

Pivin watched Jack exit the bagel place and head back toward Best Buy. *Guess he'll be in there for a while. I might as well grab a bite to eat, too.*

Best Buy had the greeter waiting at the door promptly at 8:00 a.m. TVs were first on Jack's list. They were located toward the right front of the store. Jack began walking through the aisles of various manufacturers, models, sizes, and prices.

Eagle-eye Pivin kept a close watch. He took his buttered roll and black coffee back to his car, where he could clearly see that white step van.

Jack, who was used to watching his fifteen-year-old Panasonic television, marveled at the new technology displayed all over the store.

"Sir, can I help you?"

"I think I'll look around a little, Brad." The name tag was clearly visible on the young salesman's Best Buy shirt. "I'm not sure exactly what I want."

Jack looked like a lost soul, walking back and forth in the TV aisles trying to compare one to another in size and price. The manager walked over to Brad as Jack studied the sales flyer. "Come on, Brad, make me proud today. You have only today and tomorrow, Christmas Eve, to move 'em."

"I know, boss. I'll give it my best."

"If you need anything, give me a shout."

Jack, who was lingering close by, overheard them talking. *I'll give him a sale he won't forget.*

"Hey, Brad, you have a minute?"

"Yes, sir. How can I help?"

"I'll be honest with you. I really don't know one from another. I'd like somewhere around a thirty-seven- to forty-two-inch screen, but I don't know what model. I want something decent, so it will last a few years."

"Well, this one right in front of you is on sale and it's a reputable brand. It's a forty-inch screen with high definition for only nine hundred ninety-nine dollars and ninety-nine cents. It's regularly priced at thirteen ninety-nine. You'd be saving four hundred dollars. It's a really good set and comes with a one-year warranty."

"OK, but tell me, does this one take movies too? My set at home plays VHS tapes, but I guess they've improved some since I bought mine."

"Now they take DVDs instead of tapes, but you'll need to add a DVD player." Brad was extremely polite. He knew this customer wasn't high tech.

"All righty, how do I get that DVD thing to go with the television?"

"They're right over here, sir. Follow me."

Jack gladly followed, looked at the selections, and asked Brad to pick out one that would work well with the TV model he had selected.

Brad happily obliged.

"How many do you have in stock?"

"I'll check the computer. How many did you wish to purchase?"

"Fifteen," Jack responded nonchalantly. Now that he had gotten the biggest gifts, his mind raced ahead to his next stop. He had to return the truck on time.

"Fifteen?" Brad questioned. Their voices were intertwined with the holiday music that played throughout the store.

"If you don't have fifteen of those, tell me how many you have, and then I'll have to get the rest in a similar model."

"Fifteen TVs and fifteen DVDs?" Brad repeated. This was an unbelievable sale. Wait until his manager saw this! "Do you want to purchase extended warranties or a two-year protection plan?"

"No, thanks. Just add on all the cables. It's for a sports bar. I borrowed my friend's truck to pick all this stuff up and take it there." Jack didn't want to arouse any unnecessary suspicion.

"Must be a nice place."

Jack nodded in agreement.

"Well, sir, you're in luck. The computer tells me that we do have fifteen of each. Luckily, we receive a shipment of merchandise every Wednesday." Brad's insides were jumping up and down like a little kid on a trampoline, but he had to keep his composure. After this transaction was completed, he'd let out the *yahoo*.

"Terrific!" Jack's face lit up like a kid in a toy shop. The first leg of today's mission was about to be completed, and Jack was feeling mighty happy.

Brad wrote up the bill and asked Jack to go to the cashier to pay while he gathered the entire order. They would meet him up front with all the merchandise. Jack had the money divided among several pockets, so he knew just where to dig deep. He'd get a little change from twenty thousand.

The cashier's eyebrows lifted above her big, brown eyes as she counted out $19,258 in cash. She had never done a transaction like this one.

"I never like to run up my charges," he told the cashier, to ease her surprise. "I'd much rather save up and pay in cash."

As Brad rolled one of the carts up to the checkout counter, the manager walked over to him and discreetly asked, "Did this one guy buy all these TVs and DVDs?"

"Yes, can you believe it? Says it's for a sports bar. Not bad for the first sale of the day, don't you think?"

The manager gave Brad a pat on the shoulder, "Unbelievable! I'll call Jay to assist you and get these loaded. Hey, Jay. Can you give Brad a hand?"

"No problem," Jay responded, as he headed toward the front of the store with the other flatbed pushcart.

Jack stopped. "Hey, guys, you better put on jackets. It's cold out there."

"We'll be fine."

They followed Jack's lead right to the back of the truck. Jack quickly opened up the back, hopped in, pulled the TVs forward and anchored them with the bungee cords that Richie used so the breadboxes wouldn't go flying. After the last of the TVs, DVDs, and cables were loaded, Jack put his hand in his pocket to get two twenty-dollar bills before jumping down and closing up the back door of the step van. Brad and Jay each took one of the flatbed carts and turned it around.

"Hey, guys, come over here. I want to thank you for all your help," Jack said as he tried to slip them each a twenty.

"No, thank you, sir. We're not allowed to take tips."

"Come over here. I want to show you something." Jack motioned for them to go to the side door, where they would be out of sight. "I know the rules, but this is Christmas time. I don't care what you're allowed to do. I want you to take this and go have a nice lunch or dinner, and I won't take no for an answer." Jack shoved the bills into their pants pockets. "Thanks, and have a merry."

CHAPTER THIRTY-ONE

P ivin sat in his car with the radio tuned to 1010 WINS and watched. "No new leads in the sixty-thousand-dollar Santa heist."

"Yeah, that's what you think. I just witnessed a parade of TVs. I can't wait to see the next stop. Not bad on an apartment building super's salary."

Pivin followed cautiously as Jack pulled out of the parking lot, wondering where Jack's next stop would be. He headed toward the Paramus Park Mall, turned into the parking lot, and maneuvered toward the Macy's end of the parking lot. Pivin had to get out and trail Jack as he went inside the mall and took the escalator to the lower level. There was the next stop, Toys R Us.

Jack pulled out a shopping cart and scanned the aisles. As he veered his cart into the board game section, he practically bumped into a salesperson who was on a ladder, retrieving a game from the top shelf. "Sorry, sir, I really wasn't planning on taking the ladder out from under you. I'm in sort of a jam and need help selecting some good, family-type games. You got any checkers?" For a split second, Jack visualized himself playing checkers with his dad. He wondered if stores still had those for sale.

"Yes, sir. I'll be right with you as soon as I get this box."

"Here, hand it down to me. I'm strong. Where do you want me to put it?"

"On the bottom shelf over there will be fine. This place is so busy already, and it's not even lunchtime." Jack carefully took the box and placed it on the bottom shelf where the man had indicated. "Thanks. Now, how can I help you, sir? You mentioned checkers."

"Yes, and I'll need a few other games. I see the kids with a lot of handheld stuff that they seem to get so involved with. It's like they're in another world."

"You might say that. It even happened to me—of course when I was much younger."

Jack eyeballed him for a second. *He looks like a kid himself. Couldn't be more than twenty-one.*

"Well, I'll show you some board games first."

Jack was more than happy to follow.

"Here we have checkers, Monopoly, Scrabble, Battleship, Operation—"

"Stop right there. Did you say Operation? Isn't that the game where you can take out the ankle or something, and the nose lights up like Rudolph?"

"Yeah, that's it. Which games do you want?"

"Oh, I'll take eleven of each. I'm buying for lots of kids who don't live in this area. I'd also like to get eleven of those electronic handheld games."

"Well, let's load up a cart with this stuff first, and then I'll take you over to the other corner of the store where you'll find PSPs."

"PSP's? I don't quite get that."

"Oh, sorry, that stands for PlayStation Portable. Kids love those 'cause they can take them wherever they go and play them."

"Well, I'll take eleven of those, too. My nieces and nephews will love them. I'm not their favorite uncle for nothing."

"Wish you were my uncle."

Jack's cart was overflowing as he pushed it toward the checkout counter. On his way, he spotted the big red stockings and grabbed fifteen of them. The cashier tallied a total of $2,775.58 with tax. Again, Jack pulled out cash and handed it to the wide-eyed cashier, who was obviously overwhelmed holding all those greenbacks. "You shouldn't buy things unless you have the cash is my motto," Jack lectured, as she counted and double counted. This Santa role was becoming more fun by the minute.

Pivin watched as Jack unloaded the Toys R Us bags into the van, locked it up, and headed back to the mall. "Where next?"

Jack was on a roll. He had his list and was checking it twice. The mall was the perfect place to pick up the laptop computers, the cameras, the iPods, the clock radios, and so on. He'd be able to get some little stuff tomorrow.

Pivin watched once again as the back doors of the van opened just like Jaws and consumed large deposits of boxes of various sizes and dimensions at hourly intervals. It seemed to be a feeding frenzy of sorts. *Was he a shopaholic?*

It was now one o'clock, and this watching and waiting for the next load was getting old. *How much more, Jack? Didn't you buy enough yet?*

Finally, Jack got into the driver's seat and started up the van. Slowly and carefully, he inched his way out of the spot he had occupied for the past three and a half hours. There were two vehicles competing for his spot. He didn't need to be in a fender bender, so he stopped and waited until the cars cleared a safe passage for him to exit. Jack gave them a wave of appreciation, exited the lot, and headed toward McDonald's which was on his way back to the George Washington Bridge.

The drive-through was a great invention, he thought as he got on the line. Jack rolled down the window as the voice behind the speaker welcomed him and asked what he'd like to order.

"I'll have a Whopper."

"We don't have those here. How about a value meal?"

Jack looked up and surveyed the board. "I'm real hungry, so I'll take that number three, the extra value meal. I'm always looking for good value for the almighty buck."

"Drive around to pay, sir."

"OK." Jack reached for his wallet, which he suddenly remembered he couldn't find, and pulled a ten-dollar bill from his back pocket. He never carried much money of his own. *Where did I put that wallet? I'll have to give my apartment a thorough search when I get back.*

Pivin pulled into a parking slot and waited for Jack to complete the drive-through. "Now he's got to stop for lunch. Sometimes I go all day with only a few cups of coffee and a snack or two. I don't know how long this field day is going to take. If he stops for dinner, I'm going to shoot myself."

Jack knew he had to get back before the traffic began to build. After 3:00 p.m., the cars would be bumper to bumper, and he still had to unload, tank up, and bring the truck back to Richie.

There was a steady flow of cars but no bumper to bumper traffic on the George Washington Bridge. Just as he eased into the right lane so he could exit to the Bronx, he heard a thumping sound and found it difficult to steer. *Oh no!*

Jack pulled over to the right as far as he could, put on the hazards, and got out on the right side of the van. There it was, flat as a pancake. He must have picked up a nail. *"The best laid plans of mice and men oft go awry."* That quote had stuck with him since high school. Robert Burns knew that the unexpected often happened.

Jack went back in the van, moved a few of the TVs, and freed up the spare tire, which was anchored on the left sidewall of the van. He grabbed a piece of cardboard along with the jack and lug wrench. *Might as well get to work so I can get this sleigh rollin' again. Glad it's not the double back tire. That would be a bigger pain in the neck.*

As Jack broke the lugs on the rim of the tire and jacked up the front right side, he noticed red flashing lights behind him. *Must be the bridge emergency crew.* He gave a slow backward glance as he grabbed hold of the tire and struggled to pull it off. With his eyes still on the ground as he placed the tire beside him, Jack expected to see work boots, but instead, a pair of shiny black shoes were planted on the road right next to his knee. His eyes inched upward. A long, black wool overcoat painted an unwelcome picture. His heart skipped a beat.

"Is that you? Jack…Jack La Falla?"

Jack couldn't believe his eyes. "Detective Pivin?" he gasped.

Pivin pointed to the logo on the side of the van. "I saw this bread truck stuck and thought I'd stop to help. You know, this is a dangerous place to have a breakdown. Let me give you a hand. I'll get the spare for you."

"No, no, I've got it." *The last thing I need is to have this guy snooping inside the van.* Beads of sweat were popping up again. "No need for you to get dirty." Jack tried to subdue his nervousness.

Pivin loved making a guy sweat a bit. He needed to find out what this Jack character was all about, so he continued with some casual probing. "What are you doing in Jersey with a bread truck? You got another job?"

"Oh no." Jack paused while fumbling with the lug nuts. He had to think quickly. He needed a plausible story. "I had to pick up a boiler. We got a real mess back at the apartment house. No one will deliver two days before Christmas. So I figured the best way to fix the situation was to pick it up myself. My friend loaned me his truck." Jack continued working as Pivin stood there like a mighty oak and just watched him work. The spare tire was now successfully on. Jack just had to tighten it up. Time was of the essence. *I can't believe this guy is here. What's his gig? Is he back on my case? I thought I was rid of him.*

Jack figured he might as well get right to the point. "So what brings you to New Jersey, Detective Pivin?"

"Oh, I had to visit my sister. She lives near Clifton. I always deliver Christmas presents to my nieces and nephews. You know the favorite-uncle syndrome. I like to keep up that tradition, at least while they still believe in Santa. She always puts them under the tree for me." *Jack should only know that I don't even have a sister, but if I did, I'd probably be doing that.* "So I'm on my way back home and I see this poor schnook broken down on the bridge, and I stopped to help. After all, if it was me who was in a bind, I'd hope that someone would help me out." Pivin was quite pleased with his concocted story and stood there with a slight grin.

"Yeah," Jack grunted as he lowered the jack, gave the tire a kick to make sure it was on tight, and picked up his stuff. He hoped to escape as fast as possible. "Well, thanks for stopping." As he hurried back into the right side of the van, he dropped the wrench. As Pivin picked it up, he noticed the Timberland logo on Jack's boot.

"Luckily it didn't land on my foot. That would have been a real stinger in this cold."

"Thanks, pal." *I can't believe I said* pal. *This guy is probably out to get me. Maybe he has an inside track of what happened. Coincidence that he's here? Maybe—maybe not.* Jack closed and locked the side door of the van as Pivin turned and headed back to his car. *I can't dwell on him; I have to keep going or I won't succeed.*

CHAPTER THIRTY-TWO

Normally, the fifteen-mile ride from Paramus back to Jack's neighborhood took about a half hour. As he took exit 4A toward Westchester Avenue and Hunts Point Market, he saw Pivin pass him on the left in his black Marquis and give him a thumbs-up. Jack returned the friendly gesture with a quick wave of the hand as he mouthed, "Thank you." *That guy is too sweet. I'm getting a cavity just looking at him. Wonder what he's really up to. Hopefully, I'll never know.*

Spending so much time in the car, Pivin often listened to old-ies and sang along, making up his own lyrics to familiar tunes. Sinatra's song "High Hopes" was playing. *"There goes another rubber tree plant."* But suddenly, he changed the words to *"There goes the sixty-thousand-dollar man."*

Despite the unexpected delay, Jack still got back in time to un-load the van before the kids came home from school. He dou-ble-parked, put on the flashers, unlocked the basement door, and hustled. When he got to the TVs, which were the biggest items, he decided to stack them in his living room, closer to the apartment house foyer for Christmas morning. No one would be coming to his apartment anyway; at least, he hoped not. He threw a sheet over them, just in case. As he walked back outside, he pulled the cans to the curb for the early morning pickup. He glanced up and noticed Tillie's shade being pulled down for the night. *Were the eyes and ears of 649 watching me that whole time? Funny...could that have been the same car Tillie was watching? Nah.* Jack blinked and visualized the car that he had seen pulling out. *A black Marquis. Mmm. Christmas better get here quick.*

Pivin had gotten off the next exit and circled around to Jack's neighborhood. He had to make sure he read him correctly. Jack now knew his car, so he decided to pull into one of the spaces at the Forty-first Precinct on the corner of Longwood and Southern Boulevard. He popped open his trunk; took off his black overcoat; and donned a navy ski jacket, wool hat, and gloves. He needed to take a quick stroll past 649 Longwood to see what Jack was doing. While walking on the opposite side of the street and still a distance away, Pivin noticed the white van double-parked next to the garbage can alley. Sure enough, there he was doing double-time. *Next time I move, I'll know who to hire, and it won't be the Santini Brothers.*

It was nearing 5:00 p.m. when Jack drove over to the Hess Station on Southern Boulevard to gas up. Prospect Avenue, where Richie lived, was in close proximity. As he pulled up to Richie's driveway, there he was adjusting a few holiday lights on the front of his house.

"Hey, Jack, just in time. I was beginning to worry. How'd you do with the boiler?"

"Fine, Rich. You are a lifesaver. Now I'll have to install it later today or most likely, tomorrow. Well, here are the keys. I just filled it up, so you should be good to go. Thanks again, pal." The traditional pat on the back with a hug was genuine. "Have a merry, my friend."

"You too, buddy."

Jack, thankful that he actually accomplished what he had set out to do, breathed a sigh of relief as he sauntered back home to complete his regular Thursday chores. Hopefully, there wouldn't be any special needs from the tenants. He checked his "super" mailbox and phone messages. Nothing urgent—that was good. As soon as Jack sat down on his sofa, he was overwhelmed with fatigue as if he'd been KO'd by a heavyweight champion.

Pivin walked back to his car and decided to call it a day. He needed to go home, sort things out, and try to connect the dots. He was talking to himself once again. "I could arrest him now, but he seems to be a nice guy. That man can't buy all those TVs and hang them in his tiny apartment. And what about the other stuff? What's he doing and why? Why?"

Pivin decided to take the wait-and-see approach, in spite of the fact that the actions he had witnessed today clearly indicated that Jack had lied to him—there was no boiler, and he had stockpiled the apartment house basement with tons of merchandise. When Pivin first tracked Jack down and pointed out the tear in his Santa jacket, he clearly remembered Jack's words: "Every year I play Santa for the kids in the building. I'll be using it on Christmas morning as I do every year. I like to bring a little joy into their lives."

CHAPTER THIRTY-THREE

J ack awoke earlier than usual on Friday and found himself on the sofa. He was smack in the middle of a pile of TVs. No, he wasn't dreaming; he had really done it, but he wasn't finished yet. *Yeah. This is Christmas Eve. I need to see what's left.*

His jacket and shoes were strewn on the floor next to the sofa, and he was still wearing the clothes he'd had on yesterday. He sat up and began emptying pockets and socks. *Looks like they'll be plenty of dough for stocking stuffers.* As he still had a large amount of cash, Jack's thoughts focused on the practical needs of daily living. He had faced countless struggles over the years. Jack not only knew his tenants needs, he cared. *I can't wait to see their faces on Christmas morning. This will be one day they'll never forget.*

The Duane Reed on the corner of Hunts Point Avenue and Southern Boulevard had a display of gift cards for lots of stores. He had seen them when he went to pick up some Tylenol. *Jack be nimble, Jack be quick* ran through his brain as he showered and got himself into gear. He had $27,738 left. He divided the money into pocket piles just as he had done the day before, and off he went.

As the cash flowed out, gift cards flowed in. Jack had to be quick. Today's schedule was packed. Excitement stirred within him like a volcano that was about to spew out gifts galore instead of hot, molten lava.

Jack was back before noon and unloaded. He took out a black magic marker and wrote the number of each apartment on the white felt top part of a stocking. There were fifteen of them. *Perfect!* Every step of this project had been well thought out. *So far, so good.*

These stockings wouldn't be hung by the chimney but on the stair railings. Jack spread them out across his sofa. On top of each one, he placed two MetroCards. He had purchased fifteen of them going to Bloomies and coming back from the American Girl store. He remembered instructing the attendant in the subway station booth to put the maximum on each of them. When he got the questioning "Are you sure?" look, he'd quickly responded by saying that they made great family gifts.

Next, Jack decided to purchase Visa and American Express gift cards. For some of the other types of gift cards that he knew they'd like, Jack had to do a bit of navigating in the Bronx. He needed a variety: McDonald's, Burger King, Subway, Dunkin Donuts, Target, and Key Food. Later that day, Jack shuffled them out on the top of each stocking to make sure all would receive beyond their hopes and dreams. When satisfied that all the tenants had a fair share, he placed the gift cards inside the stockings, along with some candy canes. If they were frugal, the recipients could be getting treats throughout the year. Gift cards were the next best things to greenbacks, and Jack was thankful that, for once in his life, he'd be able to dish out some joy.

Jack maneuvered through his afternoon chores quickly. He wanted to have time to check the foyer and the lights and then stack the boxes in the basement into piles before putting them into the large, black plastic bags. He had index cards labeled, one for each apartment. Individual wrapping for each box was out of the question. He had picked up fifteen large red bows to tie up each of the bags. Satisfied with Santa's sacks, he went back to his apartment to have a quick bite to eat. He flipped on the TV to watch the traditional yule log as he heated up some pigs in a blanket and popped a beer. He was so close and yet so far. There were only eight hours to go to the building's 6:00 a.m. wake-up call. He wanted everything to be perfect.

After Jack showered, he took out his suit, shirt, and tie, which he seldom wore. He stood in front of the mirror, struggling to knot his Christmas tie the way his father had shown him many years ago. *Come on, Dad, help me. Yeah, yeah, I remember, swing it around not once but twice, loop it under the back, and push it through. There it is, the half-Windsor with a dimple; thanks, Dad.* He glanced down at his parents' wedding picture on his dresser, which was right next to the snow globe. His dad's eyes seemed to be staring back at him. *Watch over me from above* was always his silent prayer. He was almost ready for midnight mass.

As Jack took out two white, legal-size envelopes, his heart began to race like a thoroughbred coming down the home stretch of the Belmont Stakes. With the $10,148 that was left, Jack knew what he would do.

The ushers greeted each person who entered the church. Holidays seemed to bring an aura of peace and joy. It would be wonderful if that existed on every day of every week. Jack watched as families were ushered to their pews and reflected on his early years. Anticipation of what the next morning might bring was evident from their smiles. Parents knew what would be under their trees, and for the first time, Jack also knew what treasures would be bestowed upon his apartment house families.

During the mass, Jack bowed his head and prayed. His giving nature was good, but the means he had taken to express it was wrong. *Oh my God, I am heartily sorry...*

As the collection basket came around, Jack hoped Father Dominick would be sitting down when he opened both envelopes. His prayers for the money to cover the cost of the much-needed repairs on the church would be answered, as well the ability to continue the programs for the neighborhood kids.

CHAPTER THIRTY-FOUR

Pivin couldn't get Jack La Falla out of his mind. He was going to check it twice just to see if he was naughty or nice. At 9:00 a.m. on the day before Christmas, Pivin was checking the license plate and the registration of the bread truck. Richie was legitimate. He wondered what was making this "super" character tick. When he first found Jack's wallet, Pivin did a background check on him, which revealed that he was clean, other than a bully incident a very long time ago. There were no La Falla family members in the area. Pivin was putting the puzzle pieces together. He knew all the reasons he should arrest Jack La Falla, but he couldn't do it this time. Perhaps he was getting soft. As he walked back to his car, the light bulb in his head turned on. "*Yes*," he yelled emphatically into the blustery wind. He needed to do some banking before heading back to his apartment to get ready for Santa.

The melancholy feeling that the holidays usually brought seemed to be lessened this year. Pivin picked up his favorite Chinese dinner with an egg roll and duck sauce, flipped on his TV to the yule log, and felt content. It didn't take long for sleep to overcome his tired body.

At 3:30 a.m., he woke up refreshed. Six hours of uninterrupted sleep was a luxury. He got dressed and headed back to the Forty-first Precinct, his home away from home.

The two cops who were on duty greeted Pivin as he entered.

"Working on Christmas Eve, Detective?"

"What, no merry Christmas? What kind of greeting is that?"

"Well, shouldn't you be home with your wife and kids?"

"You know me, Detective, twenty and out. I'm getting all the overtime I can get. That will make my pension big and fat," said Haggerty.

"You betcha," chimed in Gonzalez.

"Well, I hope you enjoy every penny of it," Pivin responded, as he walked down the hall into his office and closed the door.

Haggerty turned to Gonzalez and whispered, "Ya see that guy? He's as rich as Rockefeller. He's been on the force for over thirty years. I bet he has every penny he ever made. He squeaks when he walks."

Pivin waited for daybreak before driving over to 649 Longwood. He picked up a hot cup of coffee to keep him company while waiting for Santa.

CHAPTER THIRTY-FIVE

.

J ack walked home from church with a spring in his step. He was
psyched for the finale and set the alarm for 4:30 a.m., just in
case he fell into a deep sleep. His insides were like jumping beans.
It was as if he was the little kid waiting for Santa. He'd doze off and
then wake with a jolt, checking the time.

At 4:00 a.m., Jack headed to the basement and began gathering
the black plastic sacks. Each one was topped with a bright red bow.
He managed to carry up three at a time, and placed each one lov-
ingly around the tree that stood majestically in this transformed
lobby. The TVs were easily transported through his apartment
door, which opened into the lobby. It was getting crowded, so he
pushed them back behind the tree. Then he brought out the beautifully wrapped packages from Bloomindales and the American
Girl store. He still needed to attach the fifteen stockings to the
iron staircase railing. Duct tape would do the trick.

Jack put on the tree lights and stood back to admire his handi-
work. Stillness filled the air. The last Christmas surprise he had
had was when he received the unexpected bike. That feeling of
joy in a time of great sadness was a memory that couldn't be taken

away. Now, this one day was his way of trying to duplicate that joy for the fifteen families living under the same rooftop, struggling with their own pains and hardships.

Time was running short. It was fast approaching 6:00 a.m. He needed to check it twice to make sure he didn't forget anything. All his planning and risk taking would be over in a flash.

Jack walked back into his apartment to suit up for the big moment. *Darn it, I never did sew that tear. I'll have to remember to fix it for next year.* His cheeks were rosy, and the beard gave his face a jolly look. He checked himself out in the mirror that hung on the back of his bedroom door. *Pretty good-looking Santa.* Jack then noticed the snow globe, picked it up, and gave it shake. *It's time to pass this on.* Jack took a brown sandwich bag from the kitchen cupboard, wrote Casey's name on it, and placed the globe inside as the flakes continued to fall. He was as ready as he could ever be.

Pivin, who was sitting snugly in his black Marquis across from the building's front entrance, saw the tree lights go on in the lobby. "It must be getting close to arrival time. That Santa sure gets up early."

Jack Claus was now ready for his grand entrance. He turned up the volume on the holiday CD that he and Casey had rigged, took his brass bell, walked up the five flights, and began to bellow in his deepest voice, "Ho, ho, ho, Merry Christmas." From the fifth floor down to the first, he knocked on every apartment and rang each bell. Slowly, doors opened and heads peeked out.

"Santa's here! Santa's here!" Shouts of joy resonated throughout the building. Children tugged on their parents to hurry up and follow Santa. Yawns turned into smiles as they saw the lobby filled with presents.

"What this?"

"Did Santa really come?"

"I can't believe that Santa brought all this."

Jack played dumb to the astonished looks that surrounded him. He concentrated on the squeals of delight and couldn't have been more pleased. It was like they had all successfully done the zip line down the stairs and landed in a treasure chest filled with the most precious jewels.

"Look, this one says apartment 2B. That's us, isn't it, Santa?"

Jack nodded and sat down next to the tree. The others caught on quickly. Black plastic sacks with big red bows were being pulled in all directions.

"This one must be for us."

Santa continued to nod. This was better than he could have anticipated. The adults became children. There seemed to be lots of jumping up and down, jubilant shouts, and ear-to-ear grins.

Casey, too, was getting into it. He spotted a beautifully wrapped package. "Look, Mrs. Bauer, this one has your name on it."

"Thank you," Tillie responded.

"Go ahead, open it," Santa urged. He was watching closely as she carefully opened the wrapping. "Just tear it open."

"Oh no, I can't; the paper is too pretty. I don't want to tear it." Tillie was always the frugal one. She might be able to reuse it.

Jack wished he could bottle this joy and sprinkle it around when the chips were down. As she peered into the box, Tillie's eyes filled with tears. She looked up at Santa and mouthed the words "thank you."

Jack was pleased beyond belief. Santa exited the lobby with another "Ho, ho, ho, Merry Christmas." It was time for him to find Mr. L.

The costume change was quick. He came around and stood outside the front door to take a few deep breaths before reentering the lobby. Casey, holding the snow globe, came out to join him. He understood its significance.

"I wanted you to have it. You're the son I never had. I know you'll take good care of it. It will remind you to stay on the right path in life and become a figure others can look up to."

At the sight of Mr. L., Abby came running outside, caressing her American Girl doll. "Look, look, Mr. L." She was pointing inside the lobby. "Look what else Santa brought."

"I see, I see." Jack bent to be eye level with her, and together they peeked inside the front door. "You better get inside," Jack urged. "It's cold out here."

"We have a present for you, Mr. L. Come, come." She grabbed his hand and pulled him inside with her.

"Oh my." Jack was overcome and could barely talk. "Wow, Santa really outdid himself. You all must have been very good." It truly was an overwhelming sight to behold.

Abby ran over to her mom and was back in a flash with a giant card and a wrapped box. "Open up the cigars." There went the surprise. "Mom says you like these once in a while. They're from everyone. See, read the card."

There was a sudden hush as Jack opened it and slowly read the message. Yes, they truly were his family.

"Thank you so much. You are all so special to me. Thank you, thank you."

Jack needed air; he was choked up with emotion. With the card under his arm and the cigar box in hand, he went outside. As he was about to open the box and have a smoke, he glanced across the street and suddenly got that deer in the headlights look. *Pivin's here? He must have been staking me out this entire time. He knows.*

Pivin was leaning against his black Marquis, which was parked opposite the front door of the building. He looked left and right before crossing over to Jack.

"Merry Christmas, Jack, or is it Santa today?"

Jack stood there speechless, as if he had just seen a ghost.

"You know why I'm here, don't you, Jack?"

Jack, totally crestfallen, just stood there, lowered his head, and nodded.

"Good, that makes my job a lot easier because it really stinks when a man loses his wallet."

Jack was dumbfounded as Pivin handed him his wallet. There was no mistake; it definitely was the old, beat-up wallet that he had been looking for. He didn't know what to make of this. He was breathless, waiting for the next move.

Pivin just stood there, turning up his collar, making some idle chitchat. "Sure is cold out here, and it looks like we might get a little snow."

Jack stood there stoically, waiting for the sledgehammer to strike.

"What's in the box?"

"Cigars. Would you like one, Detective?"

"Yeah, I would."

Jack extended the opened box, and Pivin reached for one. He took it, rolled it between his fingers, and smelled it.

"Nice, thanks, Jack. And one more thing, be sure to look inside the wallet. I'm certain you'll do the right thing."

With that, Pivin turned and walked back across the street to his car. "Take care, Jack La Falla, fa la la la la, la, la, la, la."

Once in his car, Pivin lowered the driver's side window, lit the cigar, gave Jack a hand salute, and drove off.

"Hey, Mr. L., you're missing all the excitement. You coming back inside?"

"Yeah, Casey, I'll be there in a sec."

Jack opened the wallet and peered inside. There was a cashier's check made out for sixty thousand dollars.

"Who was that man?" Casey asked.

"You know, Casey, I'm not exactly sure, but I think that could have been Santa's biggest helper."

Remember, if Christmas isn't found in your heart, you won't find it under a tree.

—Charlotte Carpenter

CPSIA information can be obtained
at www.ICGtesting.com
Printed in the USA
FSOW03n2117291017
40517FS